# HOROWITZ
# HORROR

Nine nasty stories to chill you to the bone

## ANTHONY
## HOROWITZ

ORCHARD BOOKS

ORCHARD BOOKS
96 Leonard Street, London EC2A 4XD
Hachette Children's Books Australia
Level 17/207 Kent Street, Sydney, NSW 2000
ISBN  1 84362 788 4
First published in Great Britain in 1999
This edition published in 2005
Text © Anthony Horowitz 1999
The right of Anthony Horowitz to be identified as the author
of this work has been asserted by him in accordance with the
Copyright, Designs and Patents Act, 1988.
A CIP catalogue record for this book is available from the British Library.
1 3 5 7 9 10 8 6 4 2
Printed in Great Britain

# CONTENTS

# BATH NIGHT

She didn't like the bath from the start.

Isabel was at home the Saturday they delivered it and wondered how the fat, metal beast was ever going to make it up one flight of stairs, around the corner and into the bathroom. The two scrawny workmen didn't seem to have much idea either. Thirty minutes, four gashed knuckles and a hundred swear-words later it seemed to be hopelessly wedged and it was only when Isabel's father lent a hand that they were able to free it. But then one of the stubby legs caught the wallpaper and tore it and that led to another argument right in front of the workmen, her mother and father blaming each other like they always did.

'I told you to measure it.'

'I did measure it.'

'Yes. But you said the legs came off.'

'No. That's what you said.'

It was so typical of her parents to buy that bath, Isabel thought. Anyone else would have been into the West End to one of the smart department stores. Pick something out of the showroom. Out with the credit card. Delivery and free installation in six weeks and thank you very much.

But Jeremy and Susan Martin weren't like that. Ever since they had bought their small, turn-of-the-century house in Muswell Hill, north London, they had devoted their holidays to getting it just right. And since they were both teachers – he at a public school, she in a local primary – their holidays were frequent and long.

And so, the dining-room table had come from an antique shop in Hungerford, the chairs that surrounded it from a house sale in Hove. The kitchen cupboards had been rescued from a skip in Macclesfield. And their double bed had been a rusting, tangled heap when they had found it in the barn of a French farmhouse outside Boulogne. So many weekends. So many hours spent searching, measuring, imagining, haggling and arguing.

That was the worst of it. As far as Isabel could see, her parents didn't seem to get any pleasure out of all these antiques. They argued constantly – in the shops, in the market-places, even at the auctions. Once her father had got so heated he had actually broken the Victorian chamber-pot they had been fighting about and of course he'd had to buy it anyway. It was in the hall now, glued back together again, the all-too-visible cracks an unpleasant image of their twelve year old marriage.

The bath was Victorian too. Isabel had been with her parents when they bought it – at an architectural salvage yard in west London. 'End of the last century,' the dealer had told them. 'A real beauty. It's still got its own taps…'

It certainly didn't look beautiful as it squatted there on the stripped-pine floor, surrounded by stops and washers and twisting lengths of pipe. It reminded Isabel of a pregnant cow, its great white belly hanging only inches off the ground. Its metal feet curved outwards, splayed, as if unable to bear the weight. And, of course, it had been decapitated. There was a single round hole where the taps would be and beneath it an ugly yellow stain in the white enamel where the water had trickled down for perhaps a hundred years, on its way to the plug-hole below. Isabel glanced at the taps, lying next to the sink, a tangle of mottled brass that looked too big for the bath they were meant to sit on. There were two handles, marked Hot and Cold on faded ivory discs. Isabel imagined the water thundering in. It would need to. The bath was very deep.

But nobody used the bath that night. Jeremy had said he would be able to connect it up himself but in the end he had found it was beyond him. Nothing fitted. It would have to be soldered. Unfortunately he wouldn't be able to get a plumber until Monday and of course it would add another forty pounds to the bill and when he told Susan that led to another argument. They ate their dinner in front of the television that night, letting the shallow laughter of a sitcom cover the chill silence in the room.

And then it was nine o'clock. 'You'd better go to bed early, darling. School tomorrow,' Susan said.

'Yes, Mum.' Isabel was twelve but her mother sometimes treated her as if she were much younger. Maybe it came from teaching in a primary school. Although her father was a tutor at Highgate School, Isabel went to an ordinary state school and she was glad of it. They didn't allow girls at Highgate and she had always found the boys altogether too prim and proper. They were probably all gay too.

Isabel undressed and washed quickly – hands, face, neck, teeth, in that order. The face that gazed out at her from the gilded mirror above the sink wasn't an unattractive one, she thought, except for the annoying pimple on her nose...a punishment for the Mars Bar ice cream she'd eaten the day before. Long brown hair and blue eyes (her mother's), a thin face with narrow cheekbones and chin (her father's). She had been fat until she was nine but now she was getting herself in shape. She'd never be a supermodel. She was too fond of ice cream for that. But no fatty either, not like Belinda Price, her best friend at school, who was doomed to a life of hopeless diets and baggy clothes.

The shape of the bath, over her shoulder, caught her eye and she realised suddenly that from the moment she had come into the bathroom she had been trying to avoid looking at it. Why? She put her toothbrush down, turned round and examined it. She didn't like it. Her first impression had been right. It was so big and ugly with its dull enamel and dribbling stain over the plug-hole. And it seemed – it was a stupid thought but now it was there she couldn't make it go away – it seemed to be *waiting* for her. She half-smiled at her own foolishness. And then she noticed something else.

There was a small puddle of water in the bottom of the bath. As she moved her head, it caught the light and she saw it clearly. Isabel's first thought was to look up at the ceiling. There had to be a leak, somewhere upstairs, in the attic. How else could water have got into a bath whose taps were lying on their side next to the sink? But there was no leak. Isabel leaned forward and ran her third finger along the bottom of the bath. The water was warm.

'I must have splashed it in there myself,' she thought. 'As I was washing my face…'

She flicked the light off and left the room, crossing the landing to her bedroom on the other side of her parents'. Somewhere in her mind she knew that it wasn't true, that she could never have splashed water from the sink into the bath. But it wasn't an important question. In fact it was ridiculous. She curled up in bed and closed her eyes.

But an hour later her thumb was still rubbing circles against her third finger and it was a long, long time before she slept.

'Bath night!' her father said when she got home from school the next day. He was in a good mood, smiling broadly as he shuffled together the ingredients for that night's dinner.

'So you got it plumbed in then?'

'Yes.' He looked up. 'It cost fifty pounds – don't tell your mother. The plumber was here for two hours.' He smiled and blinked several times and Isabel was reminded of something she had once been told by the brother of a friend who went to the school where he taught. At school, her father's nickname was Mouse. Why did boys have to be so cruel?

She reached out and squeezed his arm. 'That's great, Dad,' she said. 'I'll have a bath after dinner. What are you making?'

'Lasagne. Your mum's gone out to get some wine.'

It was a pleasant evening. Isabel had got a part in her school play – Lady Montague in *Romeo and Juliet*. Susan had found a ten-pound note in the pocket of a jacket she hadn't worn for years. Jeremy had been asked to take a party of boys to Paris at the end of term. Good news oiled the machinery of the family and for once everything turned smoothly. After dinner, Isabel did half-an-hour's homework then kissed her parents good night and went upstairs.

To the bathroom.

The bath was ready now. Installed. Permanent. The taps with the black Hot and Cold protruded over the rim with the curve of a vulture's neck. A silver plug on a heavy chain slanted into the plug-hole. Her father had polished the brasswork, giving it a new gleam. He had put the towels back on the rail and a green bath-mat on the floor. Everything back to normal. And yet the room, the towels, the bath-mat seemed to have shrunk. The bath was too big. And it was waiting for her. She still couldn't get the thought out of her mind.

'Isabel. Stop being silly…!'

What's the first sign of madness? Talking to yourself. And the second sign? Answering back. Isabel let out a great sigh of breath and went over to the bath. She leaned in and pushed the plug into the hole. Downstairs, she could hear the television; *World in Action*, one of her father's favourite programmes. She reached out and turned on the hot tap, the metal squeaking slightly under her hand. Without pausing, she gave the cold tap a quarter-turn.

Now let's see if that plumber was worth his fifty quid.

For a moment, nothing happened. Then, deep down underneath the floor, something rumbled. There was a rattling in the pipe that grew louder and louder as it rose up but still no water. Then the tap coughed, the cough of an old man, of a heavy smoker. A bubble of something like saliva appeared at its lips. It coughed again and spat it out. Isabel looked down in dismay.

Whatever had been spat into the bath was an ugly red, the colour of rust. The taps spluttered again and coughed out more of the thick, treacly stuff. It bounced off the bottom of the bath and splattered against the sides. Isabel was beginning to feel sick and before the taps could deliver a third load of – whatever it was – into the bath, she seized hold of them and locked them both shut. She could feel the pipes rattling beneath her hands but then it was done. The shuddering stopped. The rest of the liquid was swallowed back into the network of pipes.

But still it wasn't over. The bottom of the bath was coated with the liquid. It slid unwillingly towards the plug-hole which swallowed it greedily. Isabel looked more closely. Was she going mad or was there something *inside* the plughole? Isabel was sure she had put the plug in but now it was half-in and half-out of the hole and she could see below.

There was something. It was like a white ball, turning

slowly, collapsing in on itself, glistening wet and alive. And it was rising, making for the surface...

Isabel cried out. At the same time she leant over and jammed the plug back into the hole. Her hand touched the red liquid and she recoiled, feeling it, warm and clinging, against her skin.

And that was enough. She reeled back, yanked a towel off the rail and rubbed it against her hand so hard that it hurt. Then she threw open the bathroom door and ran downstairs.

Her parents were still watching television.

'What's the matter with you?' Jeremy asked.

Isabel explained what had happened, the words tumbling over each other in their hurry to get out, but it was as if her father wasn't listening. 'There's always a bit of rust with a new bath,' he went on. 'It's in the pipes. Run the water for a few minutes and it'll go.'

'It wasn't rust,' Isabel said.

'Maybe the boiler's playing up again,' Susan muttered.

'It's not the boiler.' Jeremy frowned. He had bought it second hand and it had always been a sore point – particularly when it broke down.

'It was horrible,' Isabel insisted. 'It was like...' What had it been like? Of course, she had known all along. 'Well, it was like blood. It was just like blood. And there was something else. Inside the plug.'

15

'Oh for heaven's sake!' Jeremy was irritated now, missing his programme.

'Come on! I'll come up with you…' Susan pushed a pile of Sunday newspapers off the sofa – she was still reading them even though this was Monday evening – and got to her feet.

'Where's the TV control?' Jeremy found it in the corner of his armchair and turned the volume up.

Isabel and her mother went upstairs, back into the bathroom. Isabel looked at the towel lying crumpled where she had left it. A white towel. She had wiped her hands on it. She was surprised to see there was no trace of a stain.

'What a lot of fuss over a teaspoon of rust!' Susan was leaning over the bath. Isabel stepped forward and peered in nervously. But it was true. There was a shallow puddle of water in the middle and a few grains of reddish rust. 'You know there's always a little rust in the system,' her mother went on. 'It's that stupid boiler of your father's.' She pulled out the plug. 'Nothing in there either!' Finally, she turned on the tap. Clean, ordinary water gushed out in a reassuring torrent. No rattling. No gurgles. Nothing. 'There you are. It's sorted itself out.'

Isabel hung back, leaning miserably against the sink. Her mother sighed. 'You were making it all up, weren't you?' she said – but her voice was affectionate, not angry.

'No, Mum.'

'It seems a long way to go to get out of having a bath.'

'I wasn't...!'

'Never mind now. Clean your teeth and go to bed.' Susan kissed her. 'Good night, dear. Sleep well.'

But that night Isabel didn't sleep at all.

She didn't have a bath the following night either. Jeremy Martin was out – there was a staff meeting at the school – and Susan was trying out a new Delia Smith recipe for a dinner party the following weekend. She spent the whole evening in the kitchen.

Nor did Isabel have a bath on Wednesday. That was three days in a row and she was beginning to feel more than uncomfortable. She liked to be clean. That was her nature and as much as she tried flannelling herself using the sink, it wasn't the same. And it didn't help that her father had used the bath on Tuesday morning and her mother on Tuesday and Wednesday and neither of them had noticed anything wrong. It just made her feel more guilty – and dirtier.

Then on Thursday morning someone made a joke at school – something about rotten eggs – and as her cheeks burned, Isabel decided enough was enough. What was she so afraid of anyway? A sprinkling of rust which her imagination had turned into...something else. Susan

Martin was out that evening – she was at her Italian evening class – so Isabel and her father sat down together to eat the Delia Smith crab cakes which hadn't quite worked because they had all fallen to pieces in the pan.

At nine o'clock they went their separate ways – he to the News, she upstairs.

'Good night, Dad.'

'Good night, Is.'

It had been a nice, companionable evening.

And there was the bath, waiting for her. Yes. It *was* waiting, as if to receive her. But this time Isabel didn't hesitate. If she was as brisk and as businesslike as possible, she had decided, then nothing would happen. She simply wouldn't give her imagination time to play tricks on her. So without even thinking about it, she slipped the plug into the hole, turned on the taps and added a squirt of Body Shop avocado bubble bath for good measure. She undressed (her clothes were a useful mask, stopping her seeing the water as it filled) and only when she was quite naked did she turn round and look at the bath. It was fine. She could just see the water, pale green beneath a thick layer of foam. She stretched out her hand and felt the temperature. It was perfect: hot enough to steam up the mirror but not so hot as to scald. She turned off the taps. They dripped loudly as she remembered and went over to lock the door.

Yet still she hesitated. She was suddenly aware of her nakedness. It was as if she were in a room full of people. She shivered. 'You're being ridiculous,' she told herself. But the question hung in the air along with the steam from the water. It was like a nasty, unfunny riddle.

*When are you at your most defenceless?*

When you're naked, enclosed, lying on your back…

*…in the bath.*

'Ridiculous.' This time she actually said the word. And in one swift movement, a no-go-back decision, she got in.

The bath had tricked her – but she knew it too late.

The water was not hot. It wasn't even warm. She had tested the temperature moments before. She had seen the steam rising. But the water was colder than anything Isabel had ever felt. It was like breaking through the ice on a pond on a midwinter's day. As she sank helplessly into the bath, felt the water slide over her legs and stomach, close in on her throat like a clamp, her breath was punched back and her heart seemed to stop in mid-beat. The cold hurt her. It cut into her. Isabel opened her mouth and screamed as loudly as she could. The sound was nothing more than a choked-off whimper.

Isabel was being pulled under the water. Her neck hit the rim of the bath and slid down. Her long hair floated away from her. The foam slid over her mouth, then over her nose. She tried to move but her arms and legs wouldn't obey the signals she sent them. Her bones had frozen. The room seemed to be getting dark.

But then, with one final effort, Isabel twisted round and threw herself up, over the edge. Water exploded everywhere, splashing on to the floor. Then somehow she was lying down with foam all around her, sobbing and shivering, her skin completely white. She reached out and caught the corner of a towel, pulled it over her. Water trickled off her back and disappeared through the cracks in the floorboards.

Isabel lay like that for a long time. She had been scared...scared almost to death. But it wasn't just the change in the temperature of the water that had done it. It wasn't just the bath – as ugly and menacing as it was. No. It was the sound she had heard as she heaved herself out and jack-knifed on to the floor. She had heard it inches away from her ear, in the bathroom, even though she was alone.

Somebody had laughed.


'You don't believe me, do you?'

Isabel was standing at the bus-stop with Belinda Price; fat, reliable Belinda, always there when you needed her, her best friend. A week had passed and all the time it had built up inside her, what had happened in the bathroom, the story of the bath. But still Isabel had kept it to herself. Why? Because she was afraid of being laughed at? Because she was afraid no one would believe her? Because, simply, she was afraid. In that week she had done no work...at school or at home. She had been told off twice in class. Her clothes and her hair were in a state. Her eyes were dark with lack of sleep. But in the end she couldn't hold it back any more. She had told Belinda.

And now the other girl shrugged. 'I've heard of haunted houses,' she muttered. 'And haunted castles. I've even heard of a haunted car. But a haunted bath...?'

'It happened, just like I said.'

'Maybe you think it happened. If you think something hard enough it can often...'

'It wasn't my imagination,' Isabel interrupted.

Then the bus came and the two girls got on, showing their passes to the driver. They took their seats on the top deck, near the back. They always sat in the same place without quite knowing why.

'You can't keep coming round to my place,' Belinda said. 'I'm sorry Bella, but my mum's beginning to ask what's going on.'

'I know.' Isabel sighed. She had managed to go round to Belinda's house three nights running and had showered there, grateful for the hot, rushing water. She had told her parents that she and Belinda were working on a project.

But Belinda was right. It couldn't go on for ever.

The bus reached the traffic lights and turned on to the main road. Belinda screwed up her face, deep in thought. All the teachers said how clever she was, not just because she worked hard but because she let you see it. 'You say the bath is an old one,' she said at last.

'Yes?'

'Do you know where your parents got it?'

Isabel thought back. 'Yes. I wasn't with them when they bought it but it came from a place in Fulham. I've been there with them before.'

'Then why don't you go and ask them about it? I mean, if it is haunted there must be a reason. There's always a reason, isn't there?'

You mean...someone might have died in it or something? The thought made Isabel shiver.

'Yes. My gran had a heart attack in the bath. It didn't kill her though...'

'You're right!' The bus was climbing the hill now. Muswell Hill Broadway was straight ahead. Isabel gathered her things. 'I could go there on Saturday. Will you come too?'

'My mum and dad wouldn't let me.'

'You can tell them you're at my place. And I'll tell my parents I'm at yours.'

'What if they check?'

'They never do.' The thought made Isabel sad. Her parents never did wonder where she was, never seemed to worry about her. They were too wrapped up in themselves.

'Well…I don't know…'

'Please, Belinda. On Saturday. I'll give you a call.'


That night the bath played its worst trick yet.

Isabel hadn't wanted to have a bath. During dinner she'd made a point of telling her parents how tired she was, how she was looking forward to an early night. But her parents were tired too. The atmosphere around the table had been distinctly jagged and Isabel found herself wondering just how much longer the family could stay together. Divorce. It was a horrible word, like an illness. Some of her friends had been off school for a week and then come back pale and miserable and had never been quite the same again. They'd caught it…divorce.

'Upstairs, young lady!' Her mother's voice broke into her thoughts. 'I think you'd better have a bath…'

'Not tonight, Mum.'

'Tonight. You've hardly used that bath since it was installed. What's the matter with you? Don't you like it?'

'No. I don't…'

That made her father twitch with annoyance. 'What's wrong with it?' he asked, sulking.

But before she could answer, her mother chipped in. 'It doesn't matter what's wrong with it. It's the only bath we've got so you're just going to have to get used to it.'

'I won't!'

Her parents looked at each other, momentarily helpless. Isabel realised that she had never defied them before – not like this. They were thrown. But then her mother stood up. 'Come on, Isabel,' she said. 'I've had enough of this stupidity. I'll come with you.'

And so the two of them went upstairs, Susan with that pinched, set look which meant she couldn't be argued with. But Isabel didn't argue with her. If her mother ran the bath, she would see for herself what was happening. She would see that something was wrong...

'Right...' Susan pushed the plug in and turned on the taps. Ordinary clear water gushed out. 'I really don't understand you, Isabel,' she exclaimed over the roar of the water. 'Maybe you've been staying up too late. I thought it was only six-year-olds who didn't like having baths. There!' The bath was full. Susan tested the water, swirling it round with the tips of her fingers. 'Not too hot. Now let's see you get in.'

'Mum...'

'You're not shy in front of me, are you? For heaven's sake...!'

Angry and humiliated, Isabel undressed in front of her

mother, letting the clothes fall in a heap on the floor. Susan scooped them up but said nothing. Isabel hooked one leg over the edge of the bath and let her toes come into contact with the water. It was hot – but not scalding. Certainly not icy cold.

'Is it all right?' her mother asked.

'Yes, Mum…'

Isabel got into the bath. The water rose hungrily to greet her. She could feel it close in a perfect circle around her neck. Her mother stood there a moment longer, holding her clothes. 'Can I leave you now?' she asked.

'Yes.' Isabel didn't want to be alone in the bathroom but she felt uncomfortable lying there with her mother hovering over her.

'Good.' Susan softened for a moment. 'I'll come and kiss you good night.' She held the clothes up and wrinkled her nose. 'These had better go in the wash too.'

Susan went.

Isabel lay there on her own in the hot water, trying to relax. But there was a knot in her stomach and her whole body was rigid, shying away from the cast-iron touch of the bath. She heard her mother going back down the stairs. The door of the laundry room opened. Isabel turned her head slightly and for the first time caught sight of herself in the mirror. And this time she did scream.

And screamed.

In the bath, everything was ordinary, just as it was when her mother had left her. Clear water. Her flesh a little pink in the heat. Steam. But in the mirror, in the reflection…

The bathroom was a slaughterhouse. The liquid in the bath was crimson and Isabel was up to her neck in it. As her hand – her reflected hand – recoiled out of the water, the red liquid clung to it, dripping down heavily, splattering against the side of the bath and clinging there too. Isabel tried to lever herself out of the bath but slipped and fell, the water rising over her chin. It touched her lips and she screamed again, certain she would be sucked into it and die. She tore her eyes away from the mirror. Now it was just water. In the mirror…

Blood.

She was covered in it, swimming in it. And there was somebody else in the room. Not in the room. In the reflection of the room. A man, tall, in his forties, dressed in some sort of suit, grey face, moustache, small, beady eyes.

'Go away!' Isabel yelled. 'Go away! Go away!'

When her mother found her, curled up on the floor in a huge puddle of water, naked and trembling, she didn't try to explain. She didn't even speak. She allowed herself to be half-carried into bed and hid herself, like a small child, under the duvet.

For the first time, Susan Martin was more worried than annoyed. That night, she sat down with Jeremy and the two of them were closer than they had been for a long time as they talked about their daughter, her behaviour, the need perhaps for some sort of therapy. But they didn't talk about the bath – and why should they? When Susan had burst into the bathroom she had seen nothing wrong with the water, nothing wrong with the mirror, nothing wrong with the bath.

No, they both agreed. There was something wrong with Isabel. It had nothing to do with the bath.


The antiques shop stood on the Fulham Road, a few minutes' walk from the tube station. From the front it looked like a grand house that might have belonged to a rich family perhaps a hundred years ago: tall imposing doors, shuttered windows, white stone columns and great chunks of statuary scattered on the pavement outside. But over the years the house had declined, the plaster-work falling away, weeds sprouting in the brickwork. The windows were dark with the dust of city life and car exhaust fumes.

Inside, the rooms were small and dark – each one filled with too much furniture. Isabel and Belinda passed through a room with fourteen fireplaces, another with half-a-dozen dinner tables and a crowd of empty chairs. If they hadn't known all these objects were for sale, they could have imagined that the place was still occupied by a rich madman. It was still more of a house than a shop. When the two girls spoke to each other, they did so in whispers.

They eventually found a sales assistant in a courtyard at the back of the house. This was a large, open area, filled with baths and basins, more statues, stone fountains, wrought-iron gates and trellis-work – all surrounded by a series of concrete arches that made them feel that they could have been in Rome or Venice rather than a shabby corner of west London. The assistant was a young man with a squint and a broken nose. He was carrying a gargoyle. Isabel wasn't sure which of the two were uglier.

'A Victorian bath?' he muttered in response to Isabel's enquiry. 'I don't think I can help you. We sell a lot of old baths.'

'It's big and white,' Isabel said. 'With little legs and gold taps...'

The sales assistant set the gargoyle down. It clunked heavily against a paving stone. 'Do you have the receipt?' he asked.

'No.'

'Well...what did you say your parents' name was?'

'Martin. Jeremy and Susan Martin.'

'Doesn't ring a bell...'

'They argue a lot. They probably argued about the price.'

28

A slow smile spread across the assistant's face. Because of the way his face twisted, the smile was oddly menacing. 'Yeah. I do remember,' he said. 'It was delivered somewhere in north London.'

'Muswell Hill,' Isabel said.

'That's right.' The smile cut its way over his cheekbones. 'I do remember. They got the Marlin bath.'

'What's the Marlin bath?' Belinda asked. She already didn't like the sound of it.

The sales assistant chuckled to himself. He pulled out a packet of ten cigarettes and lit one. It seemed a long time before he spoke again. 'Jacob Marlin. It was his bath. I don't suppose you've ever heard of him.'

'No,' Isabel said, wishing he'd get to the point.

'He was famous in his time.' The assistant blew silvery grey smoke into the air. 'Before they hanged him.'

'Why did they hang him?' Isabel asked.

'For murder. He was one of those…what do you call them…Victorian axe-murderers. Oh yes…' The sales assistant was grinning from ear to ear now, enjoying himself. 'He used to take young ladies home with him – a bit like Jack the Ripper. Know what I mean? Marlin would do away with them…'

'You mean kill them?' Belinda whispered.

'That's exactly what I mean. He'd kill them and then chop them up with an axe. In the bath.' The assistant sucked at his cigarette. 'I'm not saying he did it in that bath, mind. But it came out of his house. That's why it was so cheap. I dare say it would have been cheaper still if your mum and dad had known...'

Isabel turned and walked out of the antiques shop. Belinda followed her. Suddenly the place seemed horrible and menacing, as if every object on display might have some dreadful story attached to it. Only in the street, surrounded by the noise and colour of the traffic, did they stop and speak.

'It's horrible!' Belinda gasped. 'He cut people up in the bath and you...' She couldn't finish the sentence.

'I wish I hadn't come.' Isabel was close to tears. 'I wish they'd never bought the rotten thing.'

'If you tell them...'

'They won't listen to me. They never listen to me.'

'So what are you going to do?' Belinda asked.

Isabel thought for a moment. People pushed past on the pavement. Market vendors shouted their wares. A pair of policemen stopped briefly to examine some apples. It was a different world to the one they had left behind in the antiques shop. 'I'm going to destroy it,' she said at last. 'It's the only way. I'm going to break it up. And my parents can do whatever they like...'

*

She chose a monkey-wrench from her father's tool-box. It was big and she could use it both to smash and to unscrew. Neither of her parents were at home. They thought she was over at Belinda's. That was good. By the time they got back it would all be over.

There was something very comforting about the tool, the coldness of the steel against her palm, the way it weighed so heavily in her hand. Slowly she climbed the stairs, already imagining what she had to do. Would the monkey-wrench be strong enough to crack the bath? Or would she only disfigure it so badly that her parents would have to get rid of it? It didn't matter either way. She was doing the right thing. That was all she cared about.

The bathroom door was open. She was sure it had been shut when she had glanced upstairs only minutes before. But that didn't matter either. Swinging the monkey-wrench, she went into the bathroom.

The bath was ready for her.

It had filled itself to the very brim with hot water – scalding hot judging from the amount of steam. The mirror was completely misted over. A cool breeze from the door touched the surface of the glass and water trickled down. Isabel lifted the monkey-wrench. She was smiling a little cruelly. The one thing the bath couldn't do was move. It could taunt her and frighten her but now it just had to sit there and take what was coming to it.

She reached out with the monkey-wrench and jerked out the plug.

But the water didn't leave the bath. Instead, something thick and red oozed out of the plug-hole and floated up through the water.

Blood.

And with the blood came maggots – hundreds of them, uncoiling themselves from the plug-hole, forcing themselves up through the grille and cart-wheeling crazily in the water. Isabel stared in horror, then raised the monkey-wrench. The water, with the blood added to it, was sheeting over the side now, cascading on to the floor. She swung and felt her whole body shake as the metal clanged into the taps, smashing the C of Cold and jolting the pipework.

She lifted the monkey-wrench and as she did so she caught sight of it in the mirror. The reflection was blurred by the coating of steam but behind it she could make out another shape which she knew she would not see in the bathroom. A man was walking towards her as if down a long corridor, making for the glass that covered its end.

Jacob Marlin.

She felt his eyes burning into her and wondered what he would do when he reached the mirror that seemed to be a barrier between his world and hers.

She swung with the monkey-wrench – again and again. The tap bent, then broke off with the second impact. Water spurted out as if in a death-throe. Now she turned her attention to the bath itself, bringing the monkey-wrench crashing into the side, cracking the enamel with one swing, denting the metal with the next. Another glance over her shoulder told her that Marlin was getting closer, pushing his way towards the steam. She could see his teeth, discoloured and sharp, his gums exposed as his lips were drawn back in a grin of pure hatred. She swung again and saw – to her disbelief – that she had actually cracked the side of the bath like an eggshell. Red water gushed over her legs and feet. Maggots were sent spinning in a crazy dance across the bathroom floor, sliding into the cracks and wriggling there, helpless. How close was Marlin? Could he pass through the mirror? She lifted the monkey-wrench one last time and screamed as a pair of man's hands fell on her shoulders. The monkey-wrench span out of her hands and fell into the bath, disappearing in the murky water. The hands were at her throat now, pulling her backwards. Isabel screamed and lashed out, her nails going for the man's eyes.

She only just had time to realise that it was not Marlin who was holding her but her father. That her mother was standing in the doorway, staring with wide, horror-filled eyes. Isabel felt all the strength rush out of her body like the water out of the bath. The water was transparent again, of course. The maggots had gone. Had they ever been there? Did it matter? She began to laugh.

She was still laughing half-an-hour later when the sound of sirens filled the room and the ambulance arrived.


It wasn't fair.

Jeremy Martin lay in the bath thinking about the events of the past six weeks. It was hard not to think about them – in here, looking at the dents his daughter had made with the monkey-wrench. The taps had almost been beyond repair. As it was they now dripped all the time and the letter C was gone for ever. Old water, not Cold water.

He had seen Isabel a few days before and she had looked a lot better. She still wasn't talking but it would be a long time before that happened, they said. Nobody knew why she had decided to attack the bath – except maybe that fat friend of hers and she was too frightened to say. According to the experts, it had all been stress-related. A traumatic stress disorder. Of course they had fancy words for it. What they meant was that it was her parents who were to blame. They argued. There was tension in the house. Isabel hadn't been able to cope and had come up with some sort of fantasy related to the bath.

In other words, it was his fault.

But was it? As he lay in the soft, hot water with the smell of pine bath-oil rising up his nostrils, Jeremy Martin thought long and hard. He wasn't the one who started the arguments. It was always Susan. From the day he married her, she'd insisted on...well, changing him. She was always nagging him. It was like that nickname of his at school. Mouse. They never took him seriously. She never took him seriously. Well, he would show her.

Lying back with the steam all around him, Jeremy found himself floating away. It was a wonderful feeling. He would start with Susan. Then there were a couple of boys in his French class. And, of course, the headmaster.

He knew just what he would do. He had seen it that morning in a junk shop in Hampstead. Victorian, he would have said. Heavy, with a smooth wooden handle and a solid, razor-sharp head.

Yes. He would go out and buy it the following morning. It was just what he needed. A good Victorian axe...

# KILLER CAMERA

The car-boot sale took place every Saturday on the edge of Crouch End. There was a patch of empty land there; not a car park, not a building site, just a square of rubble and dust that nobody seemed to know what to do with. And then one summer the car-boot sales had arrived like flies at a picnic and since then there'd been one every week. Not that there was anything very much to buy. Cracked glasses and hideous plates, mouldy paperback books by writers you'd never heard of, electric kettles and bits of hi-fi that looked forty years out of date.

Matthew King decided to go in only because it was free. He'd visited the car-boot sale before and the only thing he'd come away with was a cold. But this was a warm Saturday afternoon. He had plenty of time. And, anyway, it was there.

But it was the same old trash. He certainly wasn't going

to find his father a fiftieth birthday present here, not unless the old man had a sudden yearning for a five-hundred-piece Snow White jigsaw puzzle (missing one piece) or an electric coffee maker (only slightly cracked) or perhaps a knitted cardigan in an unusual shade of pink (aaaagh!).

Matthew sighed. There were times when he hated living in London and this was one of them. It was only after his own birthday, his fourteenth, that his parents had finally agreed to let him go out on his own. And it was only then that he realised he didn't really have anywhere to go. Crummy Crouch End with its even crummier car-boot sale. Was this any place for a smart, good-looking teenager on a summer afternoon?

He was about to leave when a car pulled in and parked in the furthest corner. At first he thought it must be a mistake. Most of the cars at the sale were old and rusty, as clapped-out as the stuff they were selling. But this was a red Volkswagen, L-registration, bright red and shiny clean. As Matthew watched, a smartly dressed man stepped out, opened the boot and stood there, looking awkward and ill-at-ease, as if he were unsure what to do next. Matthew strolled over to him.

He would always remember the contents of the boot. It was strange. He had a bad memory. There was a programme on TV where you had to remember all the prizes that came out on a conveyor belt and he'd never been able to manage more than two or three but this time it stayed in his mind...well, like a photograph.

There were clothes: a baseball jacket, several pairs of jeans, T-shirts. A pair of roller blades, a Tintin rocket, a paper lampshade. Lots of books; paperbacks and a brand-new English dictionary. About twenty CDs – mainly pop, a Sony Walkman, a guitar, a box of water-colour paints, a ouija board, a Game Boy...

...and a camera.

Matthew reached out and grabbed the camera. He was already aware that a small crowd had gathered behind him and more hands were reaching past him to snatch items out of the boot. The man who had driven the car didn't move. Nor did he show any emotion. He had a round face with a small moustache and he looked fed up. He didn't want to be there in Crouch End, at the car-boot sale. Everything about him said it.

'I'll give you a tenner for this,' someone said.

Matthew saw that they were holding the baseball jacket. It was almost new and must have been worth at least thirty pounds.

'Done,' the man said. His face didn't change.

Matthew turned the camera over in his hands. Unlike the jacket, it was old, probably bought second hand, but it seemed to be in good condition. It was a Pentax – but the 'x' on the casing had worn away. That was the only sign of damage. He held it up and looked through the viewfinder. About five metres away, a woman was holding up the horrible pink cardigan he had noticed earlier. He focused and felt a certain thrill as the powerful lens seemed to carry him forward so that the cardigan now filled his vision. He could even make out the buttons – silvery white and loose. He swivelled round, the cars and the crowd racing across the viewfinder as he searched for a subject. For no reason at all he focused on a large bedroom mirror propped up against another car. His finger found the shutter release and he pressed it. There was a satisfying click, it seemed that the camera worked.

And it would make a perfect present. Only a few months before, his dad had been complaining about the pictures he'd just had back from their last holiday in France. Half of them had been out of focus and the rest of them had been so overexposed that they'd made the Loire Valley look about as enticing as the Gobi Desert on a bad day.

'It's the camera,' he'd insisted. 'It's clapped out and useless. I'm going to get myself a new one.'

But he hadn't. In one week's time he was going to be fifty years old. And Matthew had the perfect birthday present right in his hands.

How much would it cost? The camera felt expensive. For a start it was heavy. Solid. The lens was obviously a powerful one. The camera didn't have an automatic rewind, a digital display or any of the other things that came as standard these days. But technology was cheap. Quality was expensive. And this was undoubtedly a quality camera.

'Will you take ten pounds for this?' Matthew asked. If the owner had been happy to take so little for the baseball jacket, perhaps he wouldn't think twice about the camera. But this time the man shook his head. 'It's worth a hundred at least,' he said. He turned away to take twenty pounds for the guitar. It had been bought by a young black woman who strummed it as she walked away.

'I'll have a look at that...' A thin, dark-haired woman reached out to take the camera but Matthew pulled it back. He had three twenty-pound notes in his back pocket. Twelve weeks' worth of shoe-cleaning, car-washing and generally helping around the house. He hadn't meant to spend all of it on his dad. Perhaps not even half of it.

'Will you take forty pounds?' he asked the man. 'It's all I've got,' he lied.

The man glanced at him, then nodded. 'Yes. That'll do.'

Matthew felt a surge of excitement and at the same time a sudden fear. A hundred-pound camera for forty quid? It had to be broken. Or stolen. Or both. But then the woman opened her mouth to speak and Matthew quickly found his money and thrust it out. The man took it without looking pleased or sorry. He simply folded the notes and put them in his pocket as if the payment meant nothing to him.

'Thank you,' Matthew said.

The man looked straight at him. 'I just want to get rid of it,' he said. 'I want to get rid of it all.'

'Who did it belong to?'

The man shrugged. 'Students,' he said – as if the one word explained it all. Matthew waited. The crowd had separated, moving on to the other stalls, and for a moment the two of them were alone. 'I used to rent a couple of rooms,' the man explained. 'Art students. Three of them. A couple of months ago they disappeared. Just did a bunk – owing two months' rent. Bloody cheek! I've tried to find them but they haven't had the decency to call. So my wife told me to sell some of their stuff. I didn't want to. But *they're* the ones who owe *me*. It's only fair…'

A plump woman pushed between them, snatching up a handful of the T-shirts. 'How much for these?' The sun was still shining but suddenly Matthew felt cold.

…*they disappeared*…

Why should three art students suddenly vanish leaving all their gear, including a hundred-pound camera, behind? The landlord obviously felt guilty about selling it. Was Matthew doing the right thing, buying it? Quickly he turned round and hurried away, before either of them changed their mind.

He had just stepped through the gates and reached the street when he heard it: the unmistakable sound of shattering glass. He turned round and looked back and saw that the bedroom mirror he had just photographed with the new camera had been knocked over. At least, he assumed that was what had happened. It was lying face-down, surrounded by splinters of glass.

The owner – a short, stocky man with a skinhead cut – bounded forward and grabbed hold of a man who had just been passing. 'You knocked over my mirror!' he shouted.

'I never went near it.' The man was younger, wearing jeans and a Star Wars T-shirt.

'I saw you! That'll be five quid...'

'Get lost!'

And then, even as Matthew watched, the skinhead drew back his fist and lashed out. Matthew almost heard the knuckles connect with the other man's face. The second man screamed. Blood gushed out of his nose and dripped down on to his T-shirt.

Matthew drew the camera close to his chest, turned and hurried away.

'It must be stolen,' Elizabeth King said, taking the camera.

'I don't think so,' Matthew said. 'I told you what he said!'

'What did you pay for it?' Jamie asked. Jamie was his

younger brother. Three years younger and wildly jealous of everything he did.

'None of your business,' Matthew replied.

Elizabeth pushed a lever on the camera with her finger-nail and the back sprang open. 'Oh look!' she said. 'There's a film in here.' She tilted the camera back and a Kodak cartridge fell into the palm of her hand. 'It's used,' she added.

'He must have left it there,' Jamie said.

'Maybe you should get it developed,' Elizabeth suggested. 'You never know what you'll find.'

'Boring family snaps,' Matthew muttered.

'It could be porn!' Jamie shouted.

'Grow up, moron!' Matthew sighed.

'You're such a nerd…!'

'Retard…'

'Come on, boys. Let's not quarrel!' Elizabeth handed the camera back to Matthew. 'It's a nice present,' she said. 'Chris will love it. And he doesn't need to know where you got it…or how you think it got there.'

Christopher King was an actor. He wasn't famous, although people still recognised him from a coffee advert he'd done two years before, but he was always in work. In this, the week before his fiftieth birthday, he was appearing as Brutus in Shakespeare's Macbeth ('the Scottish play', he called it – he said it was bad luck to mention the piece by

name). He'd been murdered six nights – and one afternoon – a week for the past five weeks and he was
beginning to look forward to the end of the run.

Both Matthew and Jamie liked it when their father
was in a London play, especially if it coincided with the
summer holidays. It meant they could spend quite a bit of
the day together. They had an old Labrador, Polonius, and
the four of them would often go out walking on
Hampstead Heath. Elizabeth King worked part-time in a
dress shop but if she was around she'd come too. They
were a close, happy family. The Kings had been married
for twenty years.

Secretly, Matthew was a little shocked about how much
money he had spent on the camera but by the time the
birthday arrived he had managed to put it behind him and
he was genuinely pleased by his father's reaction.

'It's great!' Christopher exclaimed, turning the camera
in his hands. The family had just finished breakfast and
were still sitting round the table in the kitchen. 'It's exactly
what I wanted. Automatic exposure *and* a light meter!
Different apertures…' He looked up at Matthew who was
beaming with pleasure. 'Where did you get it from, Matt?
Did you rob a bank?'

'It was second hand,' Jamie announced.

'I can see that. But it's still a great camera. Where's a film?'

'I didn't get one, Dad…' Matthew remembered the film

he'd found in the camera. It was on the table by his bed. Now he cursed himself. Why hadn't he thought to buy a new one? What good was a camera without a film?

'You haven't opened my present, Dad,' Jamie said.

Christopher put down the camera and reached for a small, square box, wrapped in Power Rangers paper. He tore it open and laughed as a carton of film tumbled on to the table. 'Now that was a great idea,' he exclaimed.

'Cheapskate,' Matthew thought, but wisely said nothing.

'Now, how does it go in…?'

'Here. Let me.' Matthew took the camera from his father and opened the back. Then he tore open the carton and started to lower the film into place.

But he couldn't do it.

He stopped.

And slid into the nightmare.

It was as if his family – Christopher and Elizabeth sitting at the breakfast table, Jamie hovering at their side - had become a photograph themselves. Matthew was suddenly watching them from outside, frozen in another world. Everything seemed to have stopped. At the same time he felt something that he had never felt in his life – a strange tingling at the back of his neck as, one after another, the hairs stood on end. He looked down at the camera which had become a gaping black hole in his hands. He felt himself falling, being sucked into it. And once he was inside, the back of the camera would be a coffin lid which would snap shut, locking him in the terrible darkness...

'Matt? Are you all right?' Christopher reached out and took the camera, breaking the spell, and Matthew realised that his whole body was trembling. There was sweat on his shoulders and in the palms of his hands. What had happened to him? What had he just experienced?

'Yes. I'm...' He blinked and shook his head.

'Are you getting a summer cold?' his mother asked. 'You've gone quite pale.'

'I...'

There was a loud snap. Christopher held up the camera. 'There! It's in!'

Jamie climbed on to his chair and stuck one leg out like a statue, showing off. 'Take me!' he called out. 'Take a picture of me!'

'I can't. I haven't got a flash.'

'We can go out in the garden!'

'There's not enough sun.'

'Well you've got to take something, Chris,' Elizabeth said.

In the end Christopher took two pictures. It didn't matter what the subjects were, he said. He just wanted to experiment.

First of all he took a picture of a tree, growing in the middle of the lawn. It was the cherry tree that Elizabeth had planted while he was appearing in Chekhov's *The Cherry Orchard* just after they were married. It had flowered every year since.

And then, when Jamie had persuaded Polonius, the Labrador, to waddle out of his basket and into the garden, Christopher took a picture of him as well.

Matthew watched all this with a smile but refused to take part. He was still feeling sick. It was as if he had been half-strangled or punched in the pit of his stomach. He reached out and poured himself a glass of apple juice. His mother was probably right. He must be going down with flu.

But he forgot about it later when two more actors from 'the Scottish play' called round and they all went out for an early lunch. After that, Christopher caught a bus into town – it was a Wednesday and he had to be at the theatre by two – and Matthew spent the rest of the afternoon playing computer games with Polonius asleep at the foot of his bed.

It was two days later that his mother noticed it.

'Look at that!' she exclaimed, gazing out of the kitchen window.

'What's that?' Christopher had been sent a new play and he was reading it before his audition.

'The cherry tree!'

Matthew walked over to the window and looked out. He saw at once what his mother meant. The tree was about three metres tall. Although the best of the blossom was over, it had already taken on its autumn colours, a great burst of dark red leaves fighting for attention on the delicate branches. At least, that was how it had been the day before.

Now the cherry tree was dead. The branches were bare, the leaves, brown and shrivelled, scattered over the lawn. Even the trunk seemed to have turned grey and the whole tree was bent over like a sick, old man.

'What's happened?' Christopher opened the kitchen door and walked out into the garden. Elizabeth followed him. He reached the tree and scooped up a handful of the leaves. 'It's completely dead!' he exclaimed.

'But a tree can't just...die.' Matthew had never seen his mother look so sad and he suddenly realised that the cherry must have been more than a tree to her. It had grown alongside her marriage and her family. 'It looks as if it's been poisoned!' she muttered.

Christopher dropped the leaves and wiped his hand on his sleeve. 'Perhaps it was something in the soil,' he said. He pulled Elizabeth towards him. 'Cheer up! We'll plant another one.'

'But it was special. *The Cherry Orchard...*'

Christopher put an arm round his wife. 'At least I took a picture of it,' he said. 'It means we've got something to remember it by.'

The two of them went back into the house leaving Matthew alone in the garden. He reached out and ran a finger down the bark of the tree. It felt cold and slimy to the touch. He shivered. He had never seen anything that looked quite so...dead.

*'I'm glad I took a picture of it...'*

Christopher's words echoed in his mind. He suddenly felt uneasy – but he didn't know why.

The accident happened the next day.

Matthew wasn't up yet. Lying in bed, he heard first the sound of the front door crashing open – too hard – and then the voices echoing up the stairs towards him.

'Liz! What is it? What's the matter?'

'Oh Chris!' Matthew froze. His mother never cried. Never. But she was crying now. 'It's Polonius...'

'What happened?'

'I don't know! I don't understand it!'

'Lizzie he's not...'

'He is. I'm sorry. I'm so sorry...' That was all she could say.

In the kitchen, Christopher made tea and listened to the cold facts. Elizabeth had walked down into Crouch End to get the newspaper and post some letters. She had taken Polonius with her. As usual, the Labrador had padded after her. She never put him on a lead. He was well-trained. He never ran into the road, even if he saw a cat or a squirrel. The truth was that, aged nearly twelve,

Polonius hardly ever ran at all.

But today, for no reason, he had suddenly walked off the pavement. Elizabeth hadn't even seen him until it was too late. She had opened her mouth to call his name when the Landrover had appeared, driving too fast round the corner. All the cars drove too fast on Wolseley Road. Elizabeth had closed her eyes at the last moment. But she had heard the yelp, the terrible thump, and she had known that Polonius could not have survived.

At least it had been quick. The driver of the Landrover had been helpful and apologetic. He had taken the dog to the vet…to be buried or cremated or whatever. Polonius was gone. He had been with the family since he was a puppy and now he was gone.

Lying in bed, Matthew listened to his parents talking and although he didn't hear all of it he knew enough. He rested his head on the pillow, his eyes brimming with tears. 'You took a picture of him,' he muttered to himself. 'A picture is all we have left.'

And that was when he knew.

At the car-boot sale, Matthew had taken a picture of a mirror. The mirror had smashed.

His father had taken a picture of the cherry tree. The cherry tree had died.

Then he'd taken a picture of Polonius…

Matthew turned to one side, his cheek coming into

contact with the cool surface of the pillow. And there it was, where he had left it, on the table by his bed. The film that he had found inside the camera when he bought it. The film that had already been exposed.

That afternoon, he took it to the chemist and had it developed.

There were twenty-four pictures in the packet.

Matthew had bought himself a Coke in a café in Crouch End and now he tore the packet open, letting the glossy pictures slide out on to the table. For a moment he hesitated. It felt wrong, stealing this glimpse into somebody else's life...like a Peeping Tom. But he had to know.

The first ten pictures only made him feel worse. They showed a young guy, in his early twenties, and somehow Matthew knew that this was the owner of the camera. He was kissing a pretty, blonde girl in one picture, throwing a cricket ball in another.

*'Art students. Three of them...'*

The man at the car-boot sale had rented part of his house to art students. And this must be them. Three of them. The camera owner. The blonde girl. And another guy, thin, with long hair and uneven teeth.

Matthew shuffled quickly through the rest of the pictures.

An exhibition of paintings. A London street. A railway station. A beach. A fishing boat. A house...

The house was different. It was like nothing Matthew had ever seen before. It stood, four storeys high, in the ruins of a garden, slanting out of a tangle of nettles and briars with great knife-blades of grass stabbing at the brickwork. It was obviously deserted, empty. Some of the windows had been smashed. The black paint was peeling in places, exposing brickwork that glistened like a suppurating wound.

Closer. A cracked gargoyle leered at the camera, arching out over the front door. The door was a massive slab of oak, its iron knocker shaped like a pair of baby's arms with the hands clasped.

Six people had come to the house that night. There was a picture of them, grouped together in the garden. Matthew recognised the three students from art school. Now they were all dressed in black shirts, black jeans. Two more men and another girl, all aged about twenty, stood behind them. One of the men had raised his arms and was grimacing, doing a vampire impersonation. They were all laughing. Matthew wondered if a seventh person had taken the picture or if it had been set to automatic. He turned over the next photograph and was taken into the house.

Click. A vast entrance hall. Huge flagstones and, in

the distance, the rotting bulk of a wooden staircase twisting up to nowhere.

Click. The blonde girl drinking red wine. Drinking it straight from the bottle.

Click. A guy with fair hair holding two candles. Behind him another guy holding a paintbrush.

Click. The flagstones again, but now they've painted a white circle on them and the guy with fair hair is adding words. But you can't read the words. They've been wiped out by the reflection from the flash.

Click. More candles. Flickering now. Placed round the circle. Three members of the group holding hands.

Click. They're naked! They've taken off their clothes. Matthew can see everything but at the same time he sees nothing. He doesn't believe it. It's madness...

Click. A cat. A black cat. Its eyes have caught the flash and have become two pinpricks of fire. The cat has sharp, white teeth. It is snarling, writhing in the hands that hold it.

Click. A knife.

Matthew closed his eyes. He knew now what they were doing. At the same time he remembered the other object that the man had been selling at the car-boot sale. He had noticed it at the time but hadn't really thought about it. The ouija board. A game for people who like to play with things they don't understand. A game for people who aren't afraid of the dark. But Matthew was afraid.

Sitting there in the cafe with the photographs spread out in front of him, he couldn't bring himself to believe it. But there could be no escaping the truth. A group of students had gone to an abandoned house. Perhaps they'd taken some sort of book with them; an old book of spells...they could have found it in an antiques shop. Matthew had once seen something like that in the shop where his mother worked: an old, leather-bound book with yellowing pages and black, splattery handwriting. A grimoire, she'd called it. The people in the photograph must have found one somewhere and, tired of the ouija board, they'd decided to do something more dangerous, more frightening. To summon up...

What?

A ghost? A demon?

Matthew had seen enough horror films to recognise what the photographs showed. A magic circle. Candles. The blood of a dead cat. The six people had taken it all very seriously – even stripping naked for the ritual. And they had succeeded. Somehow Matthew knew that the ritual had worked. That they had raised...something. And it had killed them.

*'They disappeared. Just did a bunk...'*

The man at the car-boot sale had never seen them again. Of course, they'd returned to his house, to wherever it was they rented. If they hadn't gone back, the camera would never have been there. But after that, something must have happened. Not to one of them. But to all of them.

The camera...

Matthew looked down at the prints. He had worked his way through the pile but there were still three or four pictures left. He reached out with his fingers to separate them but then stopped. Had the student who owned the camera taken a picture of the creature, the thing, whatever it was they had summoned up with their spells? Was it there now, on the table in front of him? Could it be possible...?

He didn't want to know.

Matthew picked up the entire pile and screwed them up in his hands. He tried to tear them but couldn't. Suddenly he felt sick and angry. He hadn't wanted any of this. He had just wanted a birthday present for his father and he had brought something horrible and evil into the house. One of the photographs slipped through his fingers and...

...something red, glowing, two snake eyes, a huge shadow...

...Matthew saw it out of the corner of his eye even as he tried not to look at it. He grabbed hold of the picture and began to tear it, once, twice, into ever-smaller pieces.

'Are you all right, love?'

The waitress had appeared from nowhere and stood over the table looking down at Matthew. Matthew half smiled and opened his hand, scattering fragments of the photograph. 'Yes…' He stood up. 'I don't want these,' he said.

'I can see that. Shall I put them in the bin for you?'

'Yes. Thanks…'

The waitress swept up the crumpled photographs and the torn pieces and carried them over to the bin. When she turned round again, the table was empty. Matthew had already gone.

Find the camera. Smash the camera. The two thoughts ran through his mind again and again. He would explain it to his father later. Or maybe he wouldn't. How could he tell him what he now knew to be true?

'You see, Dad, this guy had the camera and he used it in some sort of black-magic ritual. He took a picture of a demon and the demon either killed him or frightened him away and now it's *inside* the camera. Every time you take a picture with the camera you kill whatever you're aiming at. Remember the cherry tree? Remember Polonius? And there was this mirror too…'

Christopher would think he was mad. It would be better not even to try to explain. He would just take the camera and lose it. Perhaps at the bottom of a canal. His parents would think someone had stolen it. It would be better if they never knew.

He arrived home. He had his own keys and let himself in.

He knew at once that his parents had gone out. The coats were missing in the hall and, apart from the sound of hoovering coming from upstairs, the house felt empty. As he closed the front door, the hoovering stopped and a short, round woman appeared at the top of the stairs. Her name was Mrs Bayley and she came in twice a week to help Elizabeth with the cleaning.

'Is that you, Matthew?' she called down. She relaxed when she saw him. 'Your mum said to tell you she'd gone out.'

'Where did she go?' Matthew felt the first stirrings of alarm.

'Your dad took her and Jamie up to Hampstead Heath. And that new camera you bought him. He said he wanted to take their picture...'

And that was it. Matthew felt the floor tilt underneath him and he slid back, his shoulders hitting the wall.

The camera.

Hampstead Heath.

Not Mum! Not Jamie!

'What's the matter?' Mrs Bayley came down the stairs towards him. 'You look as you've seen a ghost!'

'I have to go there!' The words came out as a gabble. Matthew forced himself to slow down. 'Mrs Bayley. Have you got your car? Can you give me a lift?'

'I still haven't done the kitchen...'

'Please! It's important!'

There must have been something in his voice. Mrs Bayley looked at him, puzzled. Then she nodded. 'I can take you up if you like. But the Heath's a big place. I don't know how you're going to find them...'

She was right, of course. The Heath stretched all the way from Hampstead to Highgate and down to Gospel Oak, a swathe of green that rose and fell with twisting paths, ornamental lakes and thick clumps of woodland. Walking on the Heath, you hardly felt you were in London at all and even if you knew where you were going it was easy to get lost. Where would they have gone? They could be any-where.

Mrs Bayley had driven him down from Highgate in her rusting Fiat Panda and was about to reach the first main entrance when he saw it, parked next to a bus stop. It was his father's car. There was a sticker in the back window – LIVE THEATRE MAKES LIFE BETTER – and the bright red letters jumped out at him. Matthew had always been a little embarrassed by that stupid line. Now he read the words with a flood of relief.

'Stop here, Mrs Bayley!' he shouted.

Mrs Bayley twisted the steering wheel and there was the blare of a horn from behind them as they swerved into the side of the road. 'Have you seen them?' she asked.

'Their car. They must be up at Kenwood...'

Kenwood House. It was one of the most beautiful sights of the Heath; a white, eighteenth-century building on a gentle rise, looking down over a flat lawn and a lake. It was just the sort of place where Christopher might have gone for a walk...

*Gone to take a picture.*

Matthew scrambled out of the car, slamming the door behind him. Already he could imagine Elizabeth and Jamie with their backs to the house. Christopher standing with the camera. 'A little closer. Now smile...' His finger would stab downwards – and then what? Matthew remembered the cherry tree, colourless and dead. Polonius, who had never stepped into the road before. The mirror, smashing at the car-boot sale. A gush of blood from the fight it had provoked. Even as he ran along the pavement and swung through the first entrance to the Heath he wondered if he wasn't mad, if he hadn't imagined the whole thing. But then he remembered the pictures: the empty house, the candles.

The shadow. Two burning red eyes...

And Matthew knew that he was right, that he had imagined none of it, and that he had perhaps only minutes in which to save his father, his mother, his younger brother.

If it wasn't too late already.

Christopher, Elizabeth and Jamie weren't at Kenwood. They weren't on the terrace, or on the lawn. Matthew ran from one end of the house to the other, pushing through the crowds, ignoring the cries of protest. He thought he saw Jamie in the ornamental gardens and pounced on him – but it was another boy, nothing like his brother. The whole world seemed to have smashed (like the mirror at the car-boot sale) as he forced himself on, searching for his family. He was aware only of the green of the grass, the blue of the sky and the multicoloured pieces, the unmade jigsaw, of the people in between.

'Mum! Dad! Jamie!' He shouted their names as he ran, hoping against hope that if he didn't see them, they might hear him. He was half aware that people were looking at him, pointing at him, but he didn't care. He swerved round a man in a wheelchair. His foot came down in a bed of flowers. Somebody shouted at him. He ran on.

And just when he was about to give up, he saw them. For a moment he stood there, his breast heaving, the breath catching in his throat. Was it really them, just standing there? They looked as if they had been waiting for him all along.

But had he reached them in time?

Christopher was holding the camera. The lens cap was on. Jamie was looking bored. Elizabeth had been talking but seeing Matthew she broke off and gazed at him, astonished.

'Matthew...?' She glanced at Christopher. 'What are you doing here? What's the matter...?'

Matthew ran forward. It was only now that he realised he was sweating, not just from the effort of running but from sheer terror. He stared at the camera in his father's hand, resisting the impulse to tear it away and smash it. He opened his mouth to speak but for a moment no words came. He forced himself to relax.

'The camera...' he rasped.

'What about it?' Christopher held it up, alarmed.

Matthew swallowed. He didn't want to ask the question. But he had to. He had to know. 'Did you take a picture of Mum?' he asked.

Christopher King shook his head. 'She wouldn't let me,' he said.

'I'm too much of a mess,' Elizabeth added.

'What about Jamie?'

'What about me?'

Matthew ignored him. 'Did you take a picture of him?'

'No.' Christopher smiled, perplexed. 'What is all this, Matthew? What's the matter?'

Matthew held up his hands. 'You haven't taken a

picture of Jamie? You haven't taken a picture of Mum?'

'No.'

Then – the horrible thought. 'Did you let them take a picture of you?'

'No.' Christopher laid a hand on Matthew's shoulder. 'We've only just got here,' he said. 'We haven't taken any pictures of each other. Why is it so important anyway? What are you doing here?'

Matthew felt his knees go weak. He wanted to sink on to the grass. He felt the breeze rippling past his cheeks and a great shout of laughter welled up inside him. He had arrived in time. Everything was going to be all right.

Then Jamie spoke. 'I took a picture,' he said.

Matthew froze.

'Dad let me!'

'Yes.' Christopher smiled. 'It's the only picture we've taken.'

'But...' Just four words. But once they were spoken his life would never be the same. 'What did you take?'

Jamie pointed. 'London.'

And there it was. The entire city of London. They were standing on a hill and it lay there, spread out before them. You could see it all from here. St Paul's Cathedral. The Post Office Tower. Nelson's Column. Big Ben. That's why the Kings had come here.

For the view.

'London…?' Matthew's throat was dry.

'I got a great picture.'

'London…!'

The sun had disappeared. Matthew stood watching as the clouds closed in and the darkness rolled towards the city.

# LIGHT MOVES

I suppose my story begins with the death of a man I never met. His name was Ethan Sly and he was a journalist, the racing correspondent for the *Ipswich News* with his own column which was called Sly's Eye. He was, apparently, a thirty-a-day man – cigarettes, that is – and when he wasn't smoking he was eating, and when he wasn't eating he was drinking.

So nobody was very surprised when, at the ripe old age of forty-two, Ethan had a huge heart attack and dropped dead. In fact nobody even noticed for a couple of hours. He'd been working at his desk, typing up his tips for the Grand National, when that poor, overworked organ (his heart) had decided that enough was enough. The doctor said that it had probably happened too fast for him to feel any pain. Certainly, when they found him he just looked mildly surprised.

I learnt all this because my dad worked on the same newspaper. I've always been a bit embarrassed by this. You see, he writes the cookery column. Why cookery? Why not football or crime or even the weather report? I know I'm probably sexist and Dad's told me a hundred times that most of the famous chefs are men but still...

Anyway, he was there when they cleared out Ethan's office and that's how I ended up with the computer. And that's when all the trouble began.

Dad came back home with it the day after the funeral. He was carrying it in a big cardboard box and for a crazy moment I thought it must be a puppy or a kitten or something like that. It was the way he was cradling it in his arms, almost lovingly. He set it down gently on the kitchen table.

'Here you are, Henry,' he said. 'This is for you.'

'What is it?' Claire asked. She's my little sister, nine years old, heavily into Barbie and boy bands. We don't get on.

'It's for Henry,' my dad repeated. 'You always said you wanted to be a writer. This is to help you get started.'

I had said – once – that I wanted to be a writer. I'd just heard how much Jeffrey Archer earned. Since then the idea had stuck, and now whenever Dad introduced me to anyone, he said I was going to write. Parents are like that. They like labels.

I opened the box.

The computer was old and out of date. You could tell

just from the way that the white plastic had gone grey. The keyboard was so grubby you could hardly read some of the letters and the plastic knob had fallen off the DELETE button, leaving a metal prong showing through. There were sticky brown rings all over the hard drive where the last owner must have stood his coffee mugs while he was working. It had a colour screen and a Pentium Processor but no 3D accelerator…which meant I could kiss goodbye to all the best games.

'What's that?' My mum had come into the kitchen and was looking at the computer in dismay. We live in a modern house on an estate just outside Ipswich and my mum likes to keep it clean. She has a part-time job in a shoe shop and a full-time job as a housewife and mother. She never sits still. She's always hoovering, dusting, polishing or washing. The cooking, of course, she leaves to Dad.

'It's a computer,' I said. 'Dad gave it to me.'

'Where did you get it?' She scowled. 'It needs a wipe-down.'

'What did you get *me*?' Claire whined.

'It's for Henry. To help him with his writing,' Dad said, ignoring her. 'They were clearing out poor old Ethan's office this morning and a whole lot of stuff was going begging. I got the computer.'

'Thanks, Dad,' I said although I wasn't entirely sure about it. 'Does it work?'

'Of course it works. Ethan was using it the morning he...' But then he shrugged and fell silent.

I carried the computer up to my room and made a space for it on my desk but I didn't turn it on then and I'll tell you why. I suppose it was kind of my dad to think of me and I know he meant well but I didn't like it. It was such an ugly old machine with its grey coiling wires and heavy sockets. Although I had tucked it away in the corner, it seemed to dominate the room. Do you know what I mean? I didn't want to look at it but at the same time I couldn't keep my eyes off it. And I had a nasty feeling that the empty, dark-green glass monitor...well, I almost felt that it was staring back.

I had tea. I did my homework. I talked on the telephone to Leo (my best friend). I kicked a football around the garden and finally I had a bath and went to bed. It sounds silly but the truth is I'd put off going back to my room as long as I could. I kept on thinking of Ethan Sly. Dead and rotting in his grave. And just forty-eight hours before, his nicotine-stained fingers had been pattering across the keyboard that now sat waiting on my desk. A dead man's toy. The thought made me shiver.

I fell asleep quickly. I'm normally a heavy sleeper, but I woke up that night. Suddenly my eyes were wide open and I could feel the cool of the pillow under my head. What had woken me up? There was no sound in the room except…now I could hear a low humming noise; soft and insistent and strange. Then I realised that there was a green glow in the room. It had never been there before. It was illuminating the movie posters on my walls – not enough to make the words readable but enough to show up the pictures. I turned my head, feeling the bones in my neck click as they rotated on my spine. My left cheek touched the pillow. I looked across the room.

The computer was on. That was what was making the humming sound. The screen was lit up with a single word in large capital letters stretching across the centre.

## CASABLANCA

That made no sense to me at all. Casablanca. A city in North Africa. The title of an old film that always made my grandmother cry. Who had typed it on to the screen and why? I was more annoyed than puzzled. Obviously my dad had come into my room and turned the computer on while I was asleep. I suppose he wanted to check that it worked. But I was fussy about who came into my room. It was my private place and Mum and Dad usually respect-ed that. I didn't mind him fixing the computer. But I'd have preferred it if he'd asked.

I was too tired to get out of bed and turn it off. Instead I closed my eyes and turned my head away again to go back to sleep. But I didn't sleep. It was as if someone had thrown a bucket of iced water over me.

This is what I had seen even though my eyes had refused to believe it. This is what I was seeing now.

The computer wasn't plugged in.

The plug was lying on the carpet with the flex curled around it, a good six inches away from the socket. But the computer was still on. I put two and two together and decided I had to be dreaming. What other possibility could there be? I shut my eyes and went back to sleep.

I forgot all about the computer the next morning. I'd overslept (as usual) and I was late for school for the second time that week. It was all just a mad scrabble to get into my clothes, into the bathroom before Claire, and into school before they locked the gates. After that it was the usual school routine: maths, French, history, science...with each lesson melting into the next in the early summer sun. But then something happened and suddenly school was forgotten and the computer was right back in my mind.

It was just before the last lesson and I was walking down the corridor and Mr Priestman (biology) and Mr Thompson (English) were walking the other way. Now everybody knew that Mr Priestman was a bit of a lad; down the pub at lunch-time, smoking in the toilet since they'd made the staff-room a no-smoking area, and off to the betting shop between lessons. Well he was grinning from ear to ear as he came out of his classroom and the other teacher must have asked him what he was so pleased about because this was the fragment of conversation that I heard.

'A hundred and fifty quid.' That was the Priest.

'What was that then? A horse?' Mr Thompson asked.

'Yeah. The two o'clock at Newbury. Casablanca came in at fifteen to one.'

Casablanca.

A horse.

Ethan Sly's computer.

I don't know how I managed to get through the last lesson – it would have to be religious studies, wouldn't it? – but as soon as school was over I found my friend Leo and poured the whole thing out to him. Leo is the same age as me, fourteen, and lives in the next street. He's dark and foreign looking – his mother came from Cyprus – and he's the cleverest boy in our class.

'All right,' he said when I'd finished. 'So the ghost of this racing journalist...'

'...Ethan Sly...'

'...came back last night and haunted your Apple.'

'It's not an Apple. It's a Zircon. Or Zincom. Or something...'

'He haunted your computer and told you the result of a race that was happening today?'

'Yes, Leo. Yes. What do you think?'

Leo thought for a moment. 'I think you've had a bit too much sun.'

Maybe Leo isn't as clever as people think.

That night I did my homework at double speed, wolfed down my supper and cut out my usual argument with Claire. I went up to my room as soon as I could, closed the door and plugged the computer in. There was a switch on the front. I pressed it, then sat back and waited.

The screen lit up and a line of text stretched itself across the glass.

Zincom System. Base memory 640K. 00072K extended.

It was just the usual computer jargon – nothing unusual about that. The screen flickered a couple of times and I found myself holding my breath but then the software finished booting itself and clicked into an ordinary word-processing programme; the electronic equivalent of a blank page. I typed my name on the screen.

HENRY MARSH

The letters sat there doing nothing. I typed a line of text, even though I felt uneasy doing it.

HELLO, MR SLY. ARE YOU THERE?

Again, nothing happened and I started wondering if I wasn't behaving like an idiot. Maybe Leo was right. Maybe I had dreamt the whole incident. On the screen, the little cursor was blinking, waiting for my next input. I reached out and turned it off.

But the computer didn't turn off.

I had cut the power. The whole thing should have shut down but even as I sat there staring, two words glowed on the screen in front of me. There really was something ghostly about the letters. They didn't seem to be projected on to the glass but hung behind it, suspended in the darkness.

## MILLER'S BOY

That was the name of a horse if ever I'd heard one. I reached out for a sheet of paper and as I did so I noticed that my hand was shaking. I was actually terrified but I suppose I was too fascinated by what was happening to notice. And something else was already stirring in my mind. The computer had already predicted the winner of one race. Priestman had won one hundred and fifty pounds on Casablanca. And now here was a second horse. Maybe there would be others. Suppose I were to put money on them myself? There was no limit to the amount I could make.

I wrote the name down on the paper. At the same time the letters began to fade on the screen as if it knew they were no longer needed. A moment later they had gone.

I tracked down Leo in the first break at school the

next day. He listened to what I had to say with his usual, serious face but then he shook his head.

'Henry…' he began in a voice that told me what was about to follow.

'I'm not mad and I'm not making this up,' I interrupted. 'Look…' I had bought the *Sun* newspaper on the way to school and now I opened it at the back where the races were listed. I stabbed at the page with a finger. 'There it is,' I said, triumphantly. 'The four-forty Bunbury Fillies Handicap at Chester. Number five. Miller's Boy.'

Leo peered at the newspaper. But he couldn't argue. There it was in black and white.

'The odds are nine to two,' he said.

'That's right. So if we put two pounds on it we'll get nine pounds back.'

'If it wins.'

'Of course it'll win. That's the whole point.'

'Henry, I don't think…'

'Why don't we go down to the betting shop after school? We can go there on the way home.' Leo looked doubtful. 'We don't have to go in,' I went on. 'But it can't hurt to find out.'

'No.' Leo shook his head. 'You can go if you want to but I'm not coming. I think it's a bad idea.'

But of course he came. Why else do you think he's my best friend?

We went as soon as school was over. The betting shop was in a shabby, unfriendly neighbourhood, the sort of place where there's always graffiti on the walls and litter in the streets. I'd only ever passed it on the bus and nothing would have normally made me want to stop there. It was part of a parade of three shops and the funny thing was that you couldn't see into any of them. On the left was an off-licence, its window covered by a steel mesh. On the right was a smoke-filled café with its window coated in grease. The betting shop didn't have a window. It just had a sheet of glass painted to look like a race-track. The door was open but there were plastic strips hanging down to stop people looking in.

There was a television on inside and fortunately it was turned up high enough for us to be able to hear the commentary. Leo and I hung about on the pavement trying to look innocent as the four-twenty Fulford Handicap came to its close.

'...and it's Lucky Liz from Maryland...Lucky Liz as they come to the finishing line...it's Lucky Liz...Lucky Liz...then Maryland then the favourite, Irish Cream...'

Now, even as I was hearing this a thought was forming in my mind. I shoved my hand into my pocket and found exactly what I knew was there. Two pounds. I'd washed the car, mown the lawn and cleared the table twice for that. Slave labour! But I was thinking of what Leo had said.

If I put two pounds on Miller's Boy, I'd get nine pounds back when it won. I took the money out.

'Put it away!' Leo must have read my mind. 'You said we were only coming to look. Anyway, you're too young to bet. They wouldn't even let you in.'

And that was when Bill Garrett appeared.

Bill was famous at our school. For five years he had terrorised staff and pupils alike, never doing enough to get himself expelled but always walking close to the line. The fire that had destroyed the gymnasium had always been put down to him although nobody could ever prove anything, just like the theft of two hundred pounds from the Kosovo relief fund. It was said that when he left, aged sixteen, with no qualifications whatsoever, the teachers had thrown a party that had lasted the whole night. For a while after that, he had hung around the school gates, occasionally latching on to some of the younger kids for their dinner-money. But he had soon got bored with that and hadn't been seen for a while.

But here he was, strolling out of the café with a cigarette between his lips and an ugly look in his eyes. He must have been eighteen by now but smoking had stunted his growth. His body was thin and twisted and he smelled. He had black curly hair which fell over one eye like seaweed clinging to a rock. Leo coughed loudly and began to edge away but it was too late to run.

'What are you two doing here?' Garrett asked, recognising our uniform.

'We're lost...' Leo began.

'No we're not,' I said. I looked Garrett straight in the eye, hoping he wouldn't thump me before I got to the end of the sentence. 'We want to put a bet on a horse,' I explained.

That amused him. He smiled, revealing a set of jagged teeth, stained with nicotine. 'What horse?' he asked.

'Miller's Boy. In the four-forty at Chester.' Leo was making huge eyes at me but I ignored him. 'I want to put on two pounds.' I held out the money for Garrett to see.

'Two pounds?' he sneered. Suddenly his hand lashed out, his palm slapping up beneath my outstretched fingers. The two coins flew into the air. His hand whipped round and grabbed them. I bit my lip, annoyed with myself. They were gone and I knew it.

Garrett jiggled the coins in his hand. 'Shame to waste it on a horse,' he said. 'You can buy me a pint of beer.'

'Let's get out of here,' Leo muttered. He was just glad we were still alive.

'Wait a minute.' I was determined to see this through. 'Miller's Boy in the four-forty,' I said. 'It's going to win. Put the money on the horse and I'll let you keep half of it. Four pounds fifty each...'

'Henry...!' Leo groaned.

But I'd caught Garrett's interest. 'How can you be so sure it'll win?'

'I have a friend...' I searched for the right words. 'He knows about horses. He told me.'

'Miller's Boy?'

'I promise you, Garrett.' Inspiration struck. I held up my watch, noticing that the time was 4.35. It was now or never. 'If it loses, I'll give you my watch,' I said.

Leo rolled his eyes.

Garrett considered. You could almost see his thoughts reflected in his eyes as they churned around slowly in what passed for his brain. 'All right,' he said at last. 'You wait here. And if you move you'll be sorry.'

He loped into the betting shop, the plastic strips falling across behind him. As soon as he had gone, Leo turned to me.

'Let's run!' he gasped.

'He'd catch us.'

'We could catch a bus.'

'He knows where to find us. School...'

'I knew we shouldn't have come here.' The sadder Leo becomes, the funnier he looks. Right now I didn't know whether to laugh or cry. 'What happens if the horse doesn't win?'

'It'll win,' I muttered. 'It has to.'

The plastic strips parted and Garrett appeared holding

a blue betting ticket. 'I just got it in time,' he announced. 'The race is about to start.'

'And they're off...!' The sound from the television echoed out on to the street as the three of us stood there, Leo and me not knowing quite where to look. I wanted to get closer to the door but at the same time I didn't want to seem too eager so I stayed where I was. I could hardly hear any of the commentary and the bits I did hear didn't sound too good. It seemed that a horse called Jenny Wren had taken an early lead. Borsalino was coming up behind. I didn't even hear Miller's Boy mentioned.

But then at the very end, when the commentator's voice was at its most frantic, the magic words finally reached me.

'And it's Miller's Boy coming up on the inside. Miller's Boy! He's overtaken Borsalino and now he's moving in on Jenny Wren. Miller's Boy...can he do it?'

A few seconds later it was all over. Miller's Boy had come in first by a head. Dave Garrett looked at me long and hard. 'Wait here,' he commanded. He went back into the shop.

Leo grimaced. 'Now we're in real trouble,' he said.

'What do you mean?' I retorted. 'The horse won.'

'That's exactly what I mean. You wait and see...'

Garrett came out of the betting shop. There was a smile

on his lips but it wasn't a pleasant one. It's how you'd imagine a snake would smile at a rabbit. 'What's your name?' he asked.

'Henry Marsh.'

He held out a hand. There were three pound coins in the palm. 'Here you are, Henry,' he said. 'Three for you and six for me. That seems fair, doesn't it?'

It didn't seem fair at all but I wasn't going to argue.

'This friend of yours…' Garrett had lit another cigarette. He blew cold blue smoke into the air. 'You think I could meet him?'

'He's very shy,' I said.

'In the racing business, is he?'

'He used to be.' That was true, anyway.

Garrett placed a hand on my shoulder. His fingers dug into my collarbone, making me wince. 'It seems you and me, we need each other,' he said. His voice was friendly but his fingers were digging deep. 'You get the tips but you're too young to place the bets…'

'I don't think there will be any more tips,' I whimpered.

'Well if there are, you make sure you keep in touch.'

'I will, Garrett.'

His hand left my shoulder and clouted me across the chin hard enough to make my eyes water. 'I'm Mr Garrett now,' he explained. 'I'm not at school any more.'

He turned and walked into the off-licence. I guessed he

was going to spend the six pounds he had just won.

'Let's go,' Leo muttered.

I didn't need prompting. Together we ran to the bus stop just in time to catch a bus home. I don't think I'd ever been so glad to feel myself on the move.

That night the computer woke me up again. This time the screen carried three words.

## TEA FOR TWO

I buried my head in the pillow, trying to blot it out, but the words still burned in my mind. I'm not sure how I felt just then. Part of me was depressed. Part of me was frightened. But I was excited too. What was happening was new and strange and fantastic. And it could still make me rich. I could be a millionaire a thousand times over. Just thinking of that was enough to keep me awake all night. It would be like winning the pools every day for the rest of my life.

I didn't tell Leo about the horse. He hardly spoke to me at school the next day and I got the feeling that he didn't want to know. I had thought about telling my mum and dad but had decided against it – at least for the time being. It was my computer but if I told them, they'd probably take it away and I wasn't ready for that. Not yet.

Bill Garrett was waiting for me when I came out of school. I was on my own – Leo had got a part in the school play and had stayed behind to rehearse. At first I ignored him, walking towards the bus stop like I always did. But I wasn't surprised when he fell into step beside me. And the truth is, I wasn't even sorry. Because, you see, Garrett had been right the day before. He'd told me I needed him. And I did.

He was friendly enough. 'I wondered if you'd had any more tips,' he said.

'I might have,' I replied, trying to keep the tremble out of my voice.

'Might have?' I thought he'd turn round and punch me then. But he didn't.

'How much money have you got?' I asked him.

He dug into his pockets and pulled out a soiled five-pound note and a handful of change. 'About six quid,' he said. At a glance I could see there was nearer ten but as I told you, maths wasn't Garrett's strong point.

'I could turn that into…' I'd already checked the odds and now I made a mental calculation. 'One hundred and eighty-five pounds,' I said.

'What?'

'How much will you give me?'

'Out of a hundred and eighty-five?' He considered. 'I'll let you have thirty.'

'I want a hundred.'

'Wait a minute…' The ugly look was back on his face, although I'm not sure it had ever left it.

'That still leaves you with eighty-five,' I said. 'You put the stake down, I'll tell you the name of the horse.'

'What happens if it loses.'

'Then I'll save up and pay you back.'

We were some way from the school by now which was just as well. It wouldn't have done me any good to be seen talking to Garrett. He sneered at me in his own special way. 'How do you know I'll pay you the money if it does win?' he asked.

'If you don't, I won't give you any more tips.' I'd got it all worked out. At least, that's what I thought. Which only goes to show how wrong you can be.

Garrett nodded slowly. 'All right,' he said. 'It's a deal. What's the name of the horse?'

'Tea for Two.' Even as I spoke the words I knew that there could be no going back now. I was in this up to my neck. 'It's running in the four-fifty at Carlisle,' I said. 'The odds are twenty-five to one. It's the outsider. You can put on ten quid of your own and another three from me.' I gave him the money I had won the day before.

'Tea for Two?' Garrett repeated the words.

'Come to school on Monday with the winnings and maybe I'll have another tip for you.'

Garrett gave me an affectionate clip on the ear. It was still stinging as he scuttled off down the pavement and leapt on to a bus.

Tea for Two romped home easily. I heard the result on the radio later that evening and went to bed with a grin that stretched from ear to ear. Seeing me so cheerful, my mum decided I must be in love and Claire spent a whole hour teasing me. Well, I'd show her when I was a multi-millionaire! That night the computer stayed blank but I wasn't worried. Maybe Ethan still took the weekend off. He'd be back. For once I was actually looking forward to school and Monday morning. One hundred pounds. Put that on another horse at twenty-five to one and I'd be talking thousands.

But I didn't have to wait until Monday morning to see Garrett again. He came round the next day. He brought Leo with him. One look at the two of them and I knew I was in trouble.

Leo had a black eye and a bleeding nose. His clothes were torn and his whole face was a picture of misery. As for Garrett, he was swaggering and stalking around like a real king of the castle. I'd forgotten just how bad his reputation was. Well, I was learning the truth now and at the worst possible time. Dad was at the newspaper. Mum was taking Claire to her dancing lesson. I was in the house alone.

'Where is it?' Garrett demanded, pushing Leo through the open front door.

'What?' I asked him. But I knew.

Garrett was in the house now. I wondered if I could make a dash for the upstairs phone and call the police before he broke several of my bones. It seemed unlikely. He slammed the door.

'I'm sorry...' Leo began.

'It had to be something special,' Garrett explained. 'I knew, you see. Nobody can predict winners. Not twice in a row. Not for certain. So there had to be some sort of trick.' He lit a cigarette. My mum would kill me when she smelled the smoke. If Garrett hadn't done it first. 'I knew you'd never tell me,' he went on. 'So I popped round and visited your friend. Took him out for a little chat. Well, he didn't want to tell me neither so I had to rough him up a little bit. Made him cry, didn't I.'

'There was nothing I could do,' Leo whispered.

'This is my fault,' I said. Right then I would have given Garrett the computer just to get him out of the house.

'So then nancy-boy starts telling me this story about a ghost and a computer,' Garrett went on, puffing smoke. 'You know...I hit him some more when he told me that. I didn't believe him. But he insisted and you know what? I began to think it must be true because when I threatened to pull his teeth out he still insisted.' Garrett turned on me. 'Is it true?'

'Yes.' There seemed no point in lying.

'Where is it?'

'Upstairs. In my room. But if you go up there I'll call the police.'

'The police?' He laughed. 'You invited me in.'

He took two steps towards the stairs and I hurried over, blocking his way. Now a streak of crimson crept into his face and his eyes took on the dead look of a police Identikit picture. 'I know your parents are out,' he hissed. 'I saw them go. You get out of my way or I'll put you in hospital. You wait and see what I'll do.'

'He means it,' Leo rasped.

'It's my computer!' I cried.

Garrett threw a handful of crumpled bank-notes at me. 'No. You sold it to me for a hundred pounds. Remember?' He grinned. 'It's my computer now. You're too young to gamble anyway. It's against the law. You ought to be ashamed...'

He pushed past me. There was nothing I could do. Leo looked on miserably and I felt a bitter taste in my mouth. This was all my fault. How could I have been so stupid?

'Leo...' I began. But there was nothing I could say. I just hoped that we would still be friends when this was all over.

'You'd better go up,' Leo said.

I hurried upstairs. Garrett had already found my room and was sitting at my desk in front of the computer. He had turned it on and was waiting as the system booted itself. I stood in the doorway, watching.

'All right,' Garrett muttered. He balled his fist and struck down at the keyboard. A tangle of letters appeared on the screen. 'Come on, come on, Mr Ghost!' He slapped the side of the monitor. 'What have you got for me? Don't keep me waiting!' He hit the keyboard again. More letters appeared.

DBNOYEawES...

'Come on! Come on!' Garrett clasped the monitor in two dirty hands and pressed his face against the glass. 'You want to end up on the scrap-heap? Give me a name.'

I was certain nothing would happen. I had never asked for a horse's name to come up. It had just happened. And I had never been as greedy as this although I realised with a sick feeling in my stomach that given time I might well have become as hungry and horrible as Garrett was now. I was sure nothing would happen. But I was wrong.

The tangle of letters faded away. Two words took their place.

LIGHT MOVES

Garrett stared at the screen as if it was only now that he really believed what Leo had told him. The cigarette fell out of his lips and he giggled. His whole body was shaking. 'Light Moves.' He rolled the words on his tongue. 'Light Moves. Light Moves.' He seemed to notice me for the first time. 'Does this thing give you the odds?' he asked.

'No,' I said. I was defeated. I just wanted him to go. 'I get them in the paper.'

'I'll get them at the betting shop.' Garrett stood up. His hand curled round the flex and he yanked the plug out of the wall. The screen went blank. Then he scooped up the entire computer, holding it against his chest. 'I'll see you,' he said. 'Enjoy the hundred pounds.'

I followed him back down the stairs. Perhaps I could have stopped him but the truth is that I didn't want to. I just wanted him to go.

Leo opened the front door.

'Goodbye, suckers,' Garrett shouted.

He ran out and over the road. There was a squeal of tyres and a terrible crash. Leo and I stared at each other, then ran outside. And even now I can still see what I saw then. It's like a photograph printed into my mind.

Garrett had been hit by a large white van which had come to a halt a few yards from our front door. The driver was already out of the cabin, looking down in horror. Garrett was lying in a pool of blood that was already widening around his head. His arms and legs were splayed out so that he looked as if he were trying to swim across the tarmac of the road. But he wasn't moving. Not even to breathe.

The computer which he had been carrying when he was hit was smashed beyond repair. All the king's horses and all the king's men wouldn't put Zincom together again. Glass from the monitor was all over the road. The casing around the hard disc had split open and there were valves and wires everywhere; electronic spaghetti.

All of that was horrible, but do you know what was worse? It was the name on the side of the removals van. I saw it then and I see it just as clearly now.

### G.W. FAIRWEATHER REMOVALS LTD

And beneath that, in large red letters:

### LIGHT MOVES.

# THE NIGHT BUS

Nick Hancock and his brother, Jeremy, knew they were in trouble but what they couldn't agree on was whose fault it was. Jeremy blamed Nick, of course. Nick blamed Jonathan Saunders. And they both knew that when they finally got home – if they ever got home – their dad would blame them. But whoever was guilty, the fact was that they were stuck in the middle of London. It was five minutes to midnight. And they should have been home twenty-five minutes ago.

It was a Saturday night – and not just any Saturday night. This was October the 31st. Halloween. The two of them had been invited to a party in central London, just off Holborn. Even getting permission to go had been hard work. Nick was seventeen and was allowed out on his own. His younger brother, Jeremy, was just twelve although it was true that in another week he'd be a teenager himself. The party was being given by their cousin and that was what probably changed their parents' minds. Anybody else's party would be drugs, alcohol and vomit…at least, that was how they saw it. But this was family. How could they say no?

John Hancock, the boys' father, had finally agreed. 'All right,' he said. 'The two of you can go. But I want you home by half eleven…no arguments! Has Jonathan been invited?'

Jonathan Saunders lived just down the road. The three of them all went to the same school.

'Fine. I'll take the three of you. His mum or dad can bring you back. I'll give them a call. And Nick – you look after your brother. I just hope I'm not going to regret this…'

It had all gone horribly wrong. John Hancock had driven the three boys all the way into town. It was about a forty-minute journey from Richmond, where they all lived, out on the western edge of the city. John, who worked as a copywriter in one of the main advertising agencies, usually took the tube. But how could he take three boys across London on public transport when one of them was dressed up as a devil, one as a vampire and the last (Jonathan) as Frankenstein, complete with a bolt going through his neck?

He had dropped them off at the house near Holborn

and it had been a great party. The trouble came at the end of it, at eleven o'clock. Jonathan had said it was time to go. Nick and Jeremy had wanted to stay. And what with the noise of the music and the darkness and the crowds of other kids, they had somehow got their wires crossed.

Jonathan had left without them.

His mother, who had come to pick the three of them up, had cheerfully driven off into the night taking Jonathan but leaving the two other boys behind. Catherine Saunders was like that. She was a writer, a novelist who was always dreaming of her next plot. She was the sort of person who could drive to work only to find she'd forgotten the car. Scatty - that was her nickname. Maybe, at the end of the day, the blame was hers.

And this *was* the end of the day. It was five to twelve and Nick, dressed as the devil, and Jeremy, as Count Dracula, were feeling very small and stupid as they walked together through Trafalgar Square in the heart of London.

'We shouldn't have left,' Jeremy said, miserably.

'We had to. If Uncle Colin had seen us, he'd have called Dad and you know what that would have meant. Grounded for a month.'

'Instead of which we'll be grounded for a year...'

'We'll get home...'

'We should have been there twenty minutes ago!'

They should, of course, have taken a taxi – but there

were no free taxis around. They had thought about the tube train. But somehow they'd missed Holborn and Covent Garden tube stations and had found themselves in Trafalgar Square, in the shadow of Nelson's Column, before they knew where they were. Surprisingly, there weren't that many people around. Perhaps it was too late for the theatregoers, who would already be well on their way home, and too early for the clubbers who wouldn't even think about home until dawn. A few people glanced in the boys' direction as they made their way round the stone lions that guarded the square but quickly looked away. After all, what do you say to Dracula and the devil at five to twelve on a Saturday night?

'What are we going to do?' Jeremy complained. It felt like he'd been walking for ever. He was cold and his feet were aching.

'The night bus!' Nick spoke the words even as he saw the bus in question, parked at the far corner of the square, opposite the National Gallery.

'Where?'

'There!'

Nick pointed and there it was, an old-fashioned red bus with a hop-on, hop-off platform at the back and the magical word RICHMOND printed in white letters on the panel above the driver's cabin. The bus was the 227B. Its other destinations were printed underneath:

ST MARK'S GROVE, PALLISER ROAD, FULHAM PALACE ROAD, LOWER MILL HILL ROAD and CLIFFORD AVENUE. At least two of the names were familiar to Nick. The bus was heading west. And they had enough money for the fare.

'Come on!' Jeremy had already broken into a run, his vampire cloak billowing behind him. Nick tightened his grip on his pitchfork and ran after his younger brother, at the same time clinging on to his horns which were slipping off his head.

They reached the bus, climbed on, and took a seat about halfway along the lower deck. It was only when they were sitting down that Nick became aware that there were no lights on the bus, no other passengers, no driver and no conductor. With a sinking feeling he realised that this was one bus that wasn't going anywhere – at least not in the near future. Next to him, Jeremy was sitting back panting with his eyes half-closed. He looked at his watch. Eleven fifty-nine and counting. Ten seconds to midnight. Maybe it would be better to try again for a taxi, he decided. A taxi would have to drive through Trafalgar Square sooner or later.

'Jerry...' he said.

And, at the same moment, the lights came on, the engine rumbled into life, the bell rang and the bus lurched forward.

Nick looked up, slightly alarmed. The bus had been empty a few seconds ago, he was sure of it. But now he could see the hunched-over shoulders and dark hair of a driver, sitting in the cabin. And there was a conductor on the platform, dressed in a crumpled grey uniform that looked at least ten years out of date, feeding a paper spool into his ticket machine.

Nick and Jeremy were still the only passengers.

'Jerry...?' he whispered.

'What?'

'Did you see the driver get on?'

'What driver?' Jeremy was half-asleep.

Nick looked out of the window as the bus turned up Haymarket and made its way towards Piccadilly Circus. They passed a second bus stop with a few people waiting but the night bus didn't stop. Nor did the people waiting seem to notice it going past. Nick felt the first prickles of unease. There was something dreamlike about this whole journey; the empty bus that wasn't stopping, the driver and conductor appearing out of nowhere, even Jeremy and himself, wearing these ridiculous costumes, travelling through London in the middle of the night.

The conductor walked up the bus towards them. 'Where to?' he demanded.

Now that Nick could see the man close to, he felt all the more uneasy. The conductor looked more dead than alive.

His face was quite white, with sunken eyes and limp black hair hanging down. He was frighteningly thin. There seemed to be almost no flesh at all on his hands, which were clasped round the ticket machine; not one of the new-fangled ones that worked electronically but an old-fashioned thing with a wheel that you had to crank to spit the tickets out. But then the whole bus was completely out of date: the pattern on the seats, the shape of the windows, the cord suspended from the ceiling that you pulled to ring the bell, even the posters on the walls advertising products he had never heard of.

'Where to?' the conductor asked. He had a voice that seemed to echo before it had even left his mouth.

'Two to Richmond,' Nick said.

The conductor looked at him more closely. 'I haven't seen you before,' he said.

'Well...' Nick wasn't sure what to say. 'We don't go out this late very often.'

'You're very young,' the conductor said. He glanced at Jeremy who was now completely asleep. 'Is he your brother?'

'Yes.'

'So how did you both go?'

'I'm sorry?'

'How did you depart? What was it that...' the conductor coughed politely, '...took you?'

'My dad's car,' Nick replied, mystified.

'Tragic.' The conductor sighed and shook his head. 'So where are you going?'

'Richmond, please.'

'Lower Grove Road, I suppose. All right...' The conductor's hand rattled round in a circle and a double ticket jerked out of the machine. He handed it to Nick. 'That'll be a shilling.'

'I'm sorry?' Nick was mystified. He handed the conductor a one-pound coin and the man squinted at it distastefully. 'New currency,' he muttered. 'I still haven't got used to it. All right...' He reached into his pocket and pulled out a handful of change including several large pennies and even a threepenny piece. The last time Nick had seen one of those it had been in an antiques shop. But he didn't dare complain. Nor had he mentioned that they didn't actually want to go to Lower Grove Road. He didn't even know where it was. He didn't say anything. The bus driver walked back to the platform and left him on his own.

The bus drove round Hyde Park Corner, down through Knightsbridge and on through South Kensington. At least Nick recognised the roads and knew they were heading in the right direction. But the bus hadn't stopped; not once. Nobody had got on, not even when it was waiting at the red traffic light near Harrods. Jeremy was asleep, snoring lightly. Nick was sitting still, counting the minutes. He just wanted to be in Richmond. No matter how furious his parents would be when he finally arrived, he wanted to get back home.

And then, on the other side of Kensington, just past the Virgin Cinema on the Fulham Road, the bus finally pulled in. 'St Mark's Grove,' the conductor called out. Nick looked out of the window. There was a tall, black, metal grille on the other side of the road and a sign that he couldn't quite read in the darkness. A group of people had been waiting just in front of it and as he watched they crossed over the road and got on to the bus. The conductor pulled the cord twice and they moved off again.

Four men and three women had got on. They were all extremely well dressed, and Nick assumed they must have all come from the same dinner party. Or perhaps they'd been to the opera. Two of the men were wearing black tie with wing collars. One also had a white scarf and an ebony walking-stick. The women were in long dresses, though they wore no jewellery. They were all fairly elderly, perhaps in their sixties – but then, just as the bus picked up speed, a fifth man suddenly ran to catch up with it, reached out a hand and pulled himself on to the moving platform. Nick gasped. This was a much younger man, a motor cyclist still dressed in his leathers and carrying his helmet. But at some time he must have been involved in a terrible accident. There was a livid scar running down the side of his face and part of his head had crumpled inwards like a punctured football. The man had staring eyes and a huge grin that had nothing to do with humour. The scar had wasted his flesh, pulling one side of his lip back to expose a row of heavy, yellowing teeth. He was also dirty and smelt; the sour smell of old, damp earth. Nick wanted to stare at him but he forced himself to look away. The motor cyclist plumped himself down on a seat a few places behind him. Looking out of the corner of his eye, Nick could just make out his reflection in the glass of the window.

Curiously, the smartly dressed people seemed quite happy to have the motor cyclist in their midst.

'You only just caught it!' one of them exclaimed, nodding at the bus.

'Yeah.' The other side of his mouth twitched and for a moment the smile on his face looked almost natural. 'I got up late.'

Got up late? Nick wondered what he meant. It was, after all, a quarter past twelve at night.

'Seven tickets to Queensmill Road,' one of the women told the conductor. The handle cranked round four times, spitting out a length of white ticket.

'Queensmill Road!' the motor cyclist exclaimed. 'That's

near where I had my accident.' He touched his wounded head with his finger although to Nick, watching all this in the reflection of the window, it looked as if he actually put his finger through the wound and *into* his head. 'I collided with a mobile library,' he explained.

'Did you get booked for bad driving?' the man with the silk scarf asked and the entire company roared with laughter at the joke.

The bus stopped for a second time about five minutes later.

'Palliser Road,' the conductor called out.

At least a dozen people were waiting at the stop and they had clearly all been to the same Halloween party. They were in a lively mood as they got on to the night bus, chatting among themselves and wearing a bizarre assortment of fancy-dress costumes. Nick couldn't help looking over his shoulder as they took the seats all around them. There were two women dressed in eerie, green robes like ghosts. There were two skeletons. A boy only a few years older than Nick himself, had a knife jutting out from between his shoulders and crimson blood trickling from the corner of his mouth. An older couple had chosen, for some reason, to wear Victorian dress complete with top hat and tails for the man and flowing ballgown for the woman. Although it wasn't raining outside, both of them were dripping wet. The man noticed Nick staring at him.

'Last time I take a holiday on the *Titanic*!' he exclaimed. Nick looked the other way, embarrassed.

The people from the first bus stop soon fell into conversation with the people from the second stop and the atmosphere on the bus became quite party-like itself.

'Sir Oswald! I haven't seen you for what…? Thirty years? You look terrible!'

'Barbara, isn't it? Barbara Bennett! How is your husband? Still alive? Oh – I am sorry to hear it.'

Yes, I took the family skiing for Christmas. We had a marvellous time except unfortunately I had a massive heart attack…'

'Actually, I'm popping down to Putney to see the Fergusons. Lovely couple. Both blown up in the war…'

This went on for the next half-hour. The other passengers ignored Nick and he was grateful for it. Although he was completely surrounded by them he felt somehow different to them. He couldn't quite explain how. Perhaps it was the fact that they all seemed to know each other. They just somehow had more in common.

The night bus stopped three more times. At Queensmill Road, where the seven party-goers got off. At Lower Mill Hill Road. And finally at Clifford Avenue. By the time it left this third stop, the bus was completely full, with people standing in the corridor and on the platform. The last person to get on was more peculiar than any of them. He seemed to have just escaped from a fire. His clothes were charred and in tatters. Smoke was drifting up from his armpits and he could only nod his head in apology as the conductor tapped him on the shoulder and pointed to the 'No Smoking' sign.

If anything, the party atmosphere had intensified. All around Nick there were people talking so loudly that he could no longer hear the engine while the passengers on the upper deck had broken into song, a chorus of 'John Brown's body lies a mould'ring in the grave' which seemed to cause them great merriment. Nick tried not to stare but he couldn't help himself. As the bus approached the shops on the outskirts of Richmond, a huge, fat woman dressed, bizarrely, in a green surgical gown and sitting next to a small, bald man, suddenly turned round and blinked at him.

'What are you looking at?' she demanded.

'I wasn't...' Nick was completely tongue-tied. 'I'm sorry. It's just that I'm very late. And my parents are going to kill me!'

'It's a bit late for that, isn't it?'

'I don't know what you mean.'

'Well that's your funeral. Your funeral!' The woman roared with laughter and nudged the bald man so hard that he fell off his seat.

Laughter echoed through the night bus. There was

more singing upstairs. A man in a three-piece suit muttered a quiet 'Excuse me' and brushed a maggot off his knee. The woman next to him held a handkerchief to her nose while the woman behind her appeared to pull her nose off and hold it to her handkerchief.

Nick had had enough. The bus was approaching the centre of the town. He recognised the shops. It slowed down for a red light and that was when he decided. He grabbed hold of Jeremy, waking him up.

'Come on!' he hissed.

'What?'

'We're here!'

Half-dragging his brother, Nick got to his feet and began to push his way to the back of the bus. The light was still red but he knew it would change any second now. The other passengers didn't try to stop him, but they seemed surprised that he should be trying to get off.

'You can't leave here!' one of them exclaimed.

'We're not there yet!'

'What are you doing?'

'Come back!'

The light turned yellow, then green. The bus moved forward.

'Stop!'

'Stop him!'

The conductor, standing at the back of the platform,

lunged towards Nick and for a second he felt fingers as cold as ice clamp round his arm. 'Jump!' he shouted. Jeremy jumped off the moving bus and Nick, clinging on to his brother with one hand, was pulled with him. The conductor cried out and released him. And then they were both sprawling on the road while the night bus thundered on, rattling down the high street and on into the shadows beyond.

'What was all that about?' Jeremy said, pulling himself to his feet.

'I don't know,' Nick muttered. He knelt where he was, watching as the night bus turned a corner and disappeared, a last chorus of 'John Brown' hanging like some invisible creature in the air before swooping away and racing after it.

'I've twisted my ankle,' Jeremy groaned.

'It doesn't matter.' Nick got up and went over to his brother. 'We're home.'


'You are the most irresponsible, disobedient, bloody children I've ever met! Do you realise I was two inches away from calling the police about you? Your mother and I were sick with worry. This is the last time you go to a party on your own. In fact it's the last time you go to any party at all! I can't believe you could be so stupid...'

It was Sunday morning, breakfast, and John Hancock was still in a rage. Of course he'd been waiting for the boys when they got home, cold and exhausted, at ten to one. That night he'd rationed himself to ten minutes' shouting but after a good night's sleep it seemed he was going to rage on until lunch. In his heart, Nicholas couldn't blame him. His parents had been scared – that was the truth of it. Admittedly he was seventeen and could look after himself, but Jeremy was just twelve. And there were lots of weirdos out on the streets. Everyone knew that.

Weirdos…

'I want you to tell me more about how you got home,' his mother said. Rosemary Hancock was a quiet, sensible woman who was used to stepping in between the father and his sons when arguments flared…which they often did in the small, crowded household. She managed a bookshop in Richmond and Nick noticed she had two books with her now. One was a history of London. The other was a map book. She had brought them to the table along with the croissants and coffee.

'They already told us,' John scowled.

Rosemary ignored him. 'You said you took the 227B bus,' she said. 'An old-fashioned bus. Did it look like this?' She showed Nicholas a photograph in the book. It showed a bus just like the one he had been on.

'What does it matter what the bus looked like?' John said.

'Yes. It was just like that,' Jeremy interrupted. 'With the open door at the back.'

'And the conductor gave you old coins?'

'Yes.' Nick had left the coins beside his bed. In the daylight they had looked more than old. Some of them were rusty and coated in some sort of slime. Just looking at them had made him shudder although he couldn't say quite why.

'Do you remember where the bus stopped?' Rosemary asked. She closed the book. 'You said it went to Clifford Avenue and Lower Mill Hill Road.'

'Yes.' Nick thought back. 'It stopped in Fulham first. St Peter's Grove or something. And then at Palliser Road. And then...'

'Would it have been Queensmill Road?' Rosemary asked.

Nick stared at her. 'Yes. How do you know?'

'What are you going on about?' John demanded. 'What does it matter what the bus looked like or where it went?'

'It's just that there is no 227B bus,' Rosemary replied. 'I rang London Transport this morning while you were out getting the croissants. There is a bus that goes from Trafalgar Square to Richmond but it's the N9.' She tapped the book. 'And the bus that the boys described, the one I showed them in the photograph...it's an old Routemaster. They haven't built buses like that for thirty years and there certainly aren't any on the road.'

'Well then, how...?' John turned to look at Nick.

But Nick's eyes were fixed on his mother. The blood was draining from his face. He could actually feel it being sucked down his neck. 'But you knew the route,' he said.

'I don't know exactly what's going on here,' Rosemary began. 'Either you two boys have made the whole thing up or...I don't know...I suppose it must have been a practical joke or something.'

'Go on,' Nick said. He reached for his orange juice and took a sip. His mouth had gone dry.

'Well, it seems that last night you two did a tour of west London's cemeteries.' She opened the map book and pointed. 'St Mark's Grove, just off the Fulham Road...'

Nick remembered the tall metal grille and the sign.

'...that's Brompton Cemetery. Hammersmith Cemetery is on Palliser Road. Fulham Cemetery...that's on the Fulham Palace Road but it's opposite Queensmill Road. Putney Cemetery is on Lower Mill Hill Road and Clifford Avenue, where you say you saw that man who seemed to be smouldering or on fire – well, that's Mortlake Crematorium.'

She closed the book.

Jeremy was sitting in his seat, a piece of croissant halfway to his lips.

John Hancock stood up. 'Of course it was a practical joke,' he said. 'Now you'd better help me get Nick off the floor. He seems to have fainted.'

# HARRIET'S HORRIBLE DREAM

What made the dream so horrible was that it was so *vivid*. Harriet actually felt that she was sitting in a cinema, rather than lying in bed, watching a film about herself. And although she had once read that people only ever dream in black-and-white, her dream was in full Technicolor. She could see herself wearing her favourite pink dress and there were red bows in her hair. Not, of course, that Harriet would have *dreamt* of having a black and white dream. Only the best was good enough for her.

Nonetheless, this was one dream that she wished she wasn't having. Even as she lay there with her legs curled up and her arms tight against her sides, she wished that she could wake up and call for Fifi – her French nanny – to go and make the breakfast. This dream, which could have gone on for seconds but at the same time seemed to have stretched through the whole night, was a particularly horrid one. In fact it was more of a nightmare. That was the truth.

It began so beautifully. There was Harriet in her pink dress, skipping up the path of their lovely house just outside Bath, in Wiltshire. She could actually hear herself singing. She was on her way back from school, and a particularly good day it had been too. She had come top in spelling and even though she knew she had cheated – peeking at the words which she had hidden in her pencil case – she had still enjoyed going to the front of the class to receive her merit mark. Naturally, Jane Wilson (who had come second) had said some nasty things but Harriet had got her own back, 'accidentally' spilling a glass of milk over the other girl during lunch.

She was glad to be home. Harriet's house was a huge, white building – nobody in the school had a bigger house than her – set in a perfect garden complete with its own stream and miniature waterfall. Her brand-new bicycle was leaning against the wall outside the front door although perhaps she should have put it in the garage as it had been left out in the rain for a week now and had already begun to rust. Well, that was Fifi's fault. If the nanny had put it away for her, it would be all right now. Harriet thought about complaining to her mother. She had a special face for when things went wrong and a way of squeezing out buckets of tears. If she complained hard enough, perhaps Mummy would sack Fifi. That would be fun. Harriet had already managed to get four nannies sacked. The last one had only been there three weeks!

She opened the front door and it was then that things began to go wrong. Somehow she knew it even before she realised what was happening. But of course that was something that was often the case in dreams. Events happened so quickly that you were aware of them before they actually arrived.

Her father was home from work early. Harriet had already seen his Porsche parked in the drive. Guy Hubbard ran an antiques shop in Bath although he had recently started dabbling in other businesses too. There was a property he was developing in Bristol, and something to do with time-share apartments in Majorca. But antiques were his main love. He would tour the country visiting houses, often where people had recently died. He would introduce himself to the widows and take a look around, picking out the treasures with a practised eye. 'That's a nice table,' he would say. 'I could give you fifty pounds for that. Cash in hand. No questions asked. What do you say?' And later on that same table would turn up in his shop with a price tag for five hundred or even five thousand pounds. This was the secret of Guy's success. The people he dealt with never had any idea how much their property was worth. But he did. He once said he could smell a valuable piece even before he saw it.

Right now he was in the front living room, talking to his wife in a low, unhappy voice. Something had gone wrong. Terribly wrong. Harriet went over to the door and put her ear against the wood.

'We're finished,' Guy was saying. 'Done for. We've gone belly-up, my love. And there's nothing we can do.'

'Have you lost it all?' his wife was saying. Hilda Hubbard had once been a hairdresser but it had been years since she had worked. Even so, she was always complaining that she was tired and took at least six holidays a year.

'The whole bloody lot. It's this development. Jack and Barry have cleared out. Skipped the country. They've taken all the money and they've left me with all the debts.'

'But what are we going to do?'

'Sell up and start again, old girl. We can do it. But the house is going to have to go. And the cars…'

'What about Harriet?'

'She'll have to move out of that fancy school for a start. It's going to be a state school from now on. And that cruise the two of you were going on. You're going to have to forget about that!'

Harriet had heard enough. She pushed open the door and marched into the room. Already her cheeks had gone bright red and she had pressed her lips together so tightly that they were pushing out, kissing the air.

'What's happened?' she exclaimed in a shrill voice. 'What are you saying, Daddy? Why can't I go on the cruise?'

Guy looked at his daughter unhappily. 'Were you listening outside?' he demanded.

Hilda was sitting in a chair, holding a glass of whisky. 'Don't bully her, Guy,' she said.

'Tell me! Tell me! Tell me!' Harriet had drawn herself up as if she was about to burst into tears. But she had already decided she wasn't going to cry. On the other hand, she might try one of her ear-splitting screams.

Guy Hubbard was standing beside the fireplace. He was a short man with black, slicked back hair and a small moustache. He was wearing a checked suit with a red handkerchief poking out of the top pocket. He and Harriet had never really been close. In fact, Harriet spoke to him as little as possible and usually only to ask him for money.

'You might as well know,' he said. 'I've just gone bankrupt.'

'What?' Harriet felt the tears pricking her eyes despite herself.

'Don't be upset, my precious baby doll...' Hilda began.

'*Do* be upset!' Guy interrupted. 'There are going to be a few changes around here, my girl. I can tell you that. You can forget your fancy clothes and your French nannies...'

'Fifi?'

'I fired her this morning.'

'But I liked her!' The tears began to roll down Harriet's cheeks.

'You're going to have to start pulling your weight. By the time I've paid off all the debts we won't have enough money to pay for a tin of beans. You'll have to get a job. How old are you now? Fourteen?'

'I'm twelve!'

'Well you can still get a paper round or something. And Hilda, you're going to have to go back to hair. Cut and blow dry at thirty quid a time.' Guy took out a cigarette and lit it, blowing blue smoke into the air. 'We'll buy a house in Bletchley or somewhere. One bedroom is all we can afford.'

'So where will I sleep?' Harriet quavered.

'You can sleep in the bath.'

And that was what did it. The tears were pouring now – not just out of Harriet's eyes but also, more revoltingly, out of her nose. At the same time she let out one of her loudest, shrillest screams. 'I won't! I won't! I won't!' she yelled. 'I'm not leaving this house and I'm not sleeping in the bath. This is all your fault, Daddy. I hate you and I've always hated you and I hate Mummy too and I am going on my cruise and if you stop me I'll report you to the

NSPCC and the police and I'll tell everyone that you steal things from old ladies and you never pay any tax and you'll go to prison and see if I care!'

Harriet was screaming so loudly that she had almost suffocated herself. She stopped and sucked in a great breath of air, then turned on her heel and flounced out of the room, slamming the door behind her. Even as she went, she heard her father mutter, 'We're going to have to do something about that girl.'

But then she was gone.

And then, as is so often the way in dreams, it was the next day, or perhaps the day after, and she was sitting at the breakfast table with her mother who was eating a bowl of low-fat muesli and reading the *Sun* when her father came into the kitchen.

'Good morning,' he said.

Harriet ignored him.

'All right,' Guy said. 'I've listened to what you had to say and I've talked things over with your mother and it does seem that we're going to have to come to a new arrangement.'

Harriet helped herself to a third crumpet and smothered it in butter. She was being very prim and lady-like, she thought. Very grown up. The effect was only spoiled when melted butter dribbled down her chin.

'We're moving,' Guy went on. 'But you're right. There

isn't going to be room for you in the new set-up. You're too much of a little miss.'

'Guy…' Hilda muttered, disapprovingly.

Her husband ignored her. 'I've spoken to your Uncle Algernon,' he said. 'He's agreed to take you.'

'I don't have an Uncle Algernon,' Harriet sniffed.

'He's not really your uncle. But he's an old friend of the family. He runs a restaurant in London. The 'Sawney Bean'. That's what it's called.'

'That's a stupid name for a restaurant,' Harriet said.

'Stupid or not, it's made a bomb. He's raking it in. And he needs a young girl like you. Don't ask me what for! Anyway, I've telephoned him today and he's driving down to pick you up. You can go with him. And maybe one day when we've sorted ourselves out…'

'I'll miss my little Harry-Warry!' Hilda moaned.

'You won't miss her at all! You've been too busy playing bridge and having your toes manicured to look after her properly. Maybe that's why she's turned into such a spoilt little so-and-so. But it's too late now. He'll be here soon. You'd better go and pack a bag.'

'My baby!' This time it was Hilda who began to cry, her tears dripping into her muesli.

'I'll take two bags,' Harriet said. 'And you'd better give me some pocket money too. Six months in advance!'

Uncle Algernon turned up at midday. After what her

father had said, Harriet had expected him to drive a Rolls-Royce or at the very least a Jaguar and was disappointed by her first sight of him, rattling up the drive in a rather battered white van with the restaurant name, SAWNEY BEAN, written in blood-red letters on the side.

The van stopped and a figure got out, almost impossibly, from the front seat. He was so tall that Harriet was unsure how he had ever managed to fit inside. As he straightened up, he was much taller than the van itself, his bald head higher even than the aerial on the roof. He was also revoltingly thin. It was as if a normal human being had been put on a rack and stretched. His legs and his arms, hanging loose by his side, seemed to be made of elastic. His face was unusually repulsive. Although he had no hair on his head, he had big, bushy eyebrows which didn't quite fit over his small, glistening eyes. His skin was the colour of a ping-pong ball. His whole head was roughly the same shape. He was wearing a black coat with a fur collar round his neck and gleaming black shoes which squeaked when he walked.

Guy Hubbard was the first one out to greet him. 'Hello, Archie!' he exclaimed. The two men shook hands. 'How's business?'

'Busy. Very busy.' Algernon had a soft, low voice that reminded Harriet of an undertaker. 'I can't hang around, Guy. I have to be back in town by lunch. Lunch!' He licked his lips with a wet, pink tongue. 'Fully booked today. And tomorrow. And all week. Sawney Bean has been more successful than I would ever have imagined.'

'Coining it in, I bet.'

'You could say that.'

'So have you got it then?'

Algernon smiled and reached into the pocket of his coat, pulling out a crumpled brown envelope which he handed to Guy. Harriet watched, puzzled, from the front door. She knew what brown envelopes meant when her father was concerned. This man, Algernon, was obviously giving him money – and lots of it from the size of the envelope. But he was the one who was taking her away to look after her. So shouldn't Guy have been paying *him*?

Guy pocketed the money.

'So where is she?' Algernon asked.

'Harriet!' Guy called.

Harriet picked up her two suitcases and stepped out of the house for the last time. 'I'm here,' she said. 'But I hope you're not expecting me to travel in that perfectly horrid little van…'

Guy scowled. But it seemed that Algernon hadn't heard her. He was staring at her with something in his eyes that was hard to define. He was certainly pleased by what he saw. He was happy. But there was something else.

Hunger? Harriet could almost feel the eyes running up and down her body.

She put the cases down and grimaced as he ran a finger along the side of her face. 'Oh yes,' he breathed. 'She's perfect. First class. She'll do very well.'

'What will I do very well?' Harriet demanded.

'None of your business,' Guy replied.

Meanwhile, Hilda had come out on to the drive. She was trembling and, Harriet noticed, refused to look at the new arrival.

'It's time to go,' Guy said.

Algernon smiled at Harriet. He had dreadful teeth. They were yellow and uneven and – worse – strangely pointy. They were more like the teeth of an animal. 'Get in,' he said. 'It's a long drive.'

Hilda broke out in fresh tears. 'Aren't you going to kiss me goodbye?' she wailed.

'No,' Harriet replied.

'Goodbye,' Guy said. He wanted to get this over with as soon as possible.

Harriet climbed into the van while Algernon placed her cases in the back. The front seat was covered in cheap plastic and it was torn in places, the stuffing oozing through. There was also a mess on the floor; sweet wrappers, old invoices and an empty cigarette pack. She tried to lower the window but the handle wouldn't turn.

'Goodbye, Mummy! Goodbye, Dad!' she called through the glass. 'I never liked it here and I'm not sorry I'm going. Maybe I'll see you again when I'm grown up.'

'I doubt it...' Had her father really said that? That was certainly what it sounded like. Harriet turned her head away in contempt.

Algernon had climbed in next to her. He had to coil his whole body up to fit in and his head still touched the roof. He started the engine up and a moment later the van was driving away. Harriet didn't look back. She didn't want her parents to think she was going to miss them.

The two of them didn't speak until they had reached the M4 motorway and begun the long journey east towards the city. Harriet had looked for the radio, hoping to listen to music. But it had been stolen, the broken wires hanging out of the dashboard. She was aware of Algernon examining her out of the corner of his eye even as he drove and when this became too irritating she finally spoke.

'So tell me about this restaurant of yours,' she said.

'What do you want to know?' Algernon asked.

'I don't know...'

'It's very exclusive,' Algernon began. 'In fact it's so exclusive that very few people know about it. Even so, it is full every night. We never advertise but word gets around. You could say that it's word of mouth. Yes. Word of mouth is very much what we're about.'

There was something creepy about the way he said that. Once again his tongue slid over his lips. He smiled to himself, as if at some secret joke.

'Is it an expensive restaurant?' Harriet asked.

'Oh yes. It is the most expensive restaurant in London. Do you know how much dinner for two at my restaurant would cost you?'

Harriet shrugged.

'Five hundred pounds. And that's not including the wine.'

'That's crazy!' Harriet scowled. 'Nobody would pay that much for a dinner for two.'

'My clients are more than happy to pay. You see...' Algernon smiled again. His eyes never left the road. 'There are people who make lots of money in their lives. Film stars and writers. Investment bankers and businessmen. They have millions and millions of pounds and they have to spend it on something. These people think nothing of spending a hundred pounds on a few spoonfuls of caviar. They'll spend a thousand pounds on a single bottle of wine! They go to all the smartest restaurants and they don't care how much they pay as long as their meal is cooked by a famous cook, ideally with the menu written in French and all the ingredients flown, at huge expense, from all around the world. Are you with me, my dear?'

'Don't call me "my dear",' Harriet said.

Algernon chuckled softly. 'But of course there comes a time,' he went on, 'when they've eaten everything there is to be had. The best smoked salmon and the finest fillet steak. There are only so many ingredients in the world, my dear, and soon they find they've tasted them all. Oh yes, there are a thousand ways to prepare them. Pigeon's breast with marmalade and foie gras. Smoked sea bass with shallots and Shitaki mushrooms. But there comes a time when they feel they've had it all. When their appetites become jaded. When they're looking for a completely different eating experience. And that's when they come to Sawney Bean.'

'Why did you give the restaurant such a stupid name?' Harriet asked.

'It's named after a real person,' Algernon replied. He didn't seem ruffled at all even though Harriet had been purposefully trying to annoy him. 'Sawney Bean lived in Scotland at the start of the century. He had unusual tastes…'

'I hope you're not expecting me to work in this restaurant.'

'To work?' Algernon smiled. 'Oh no. But I do expect you to appear in it. In fact, I'm planning to introduce you at dinner tonight…'

The dream shifted forward and suddenly they were in

London, making their way down the King's Road, in Chelsea. And there was the restaurant! Harriet saw a small, white-bricked building with the name written in red letters above the door. The restaurant had no window and there was no menu on display. In fact, if Algernon hadn't pointed it out she wouldn't have noticed it at all. He indicated and the van turned into a narrow alley, running behind the building.

'Is this where you live?' Harriet asked. 'Is this where I'm going to live?'

'For the next few hours,' Algernon replied. He pulled up at the end of the alley in a small courtyard surrounded on all sides by high brick walls. There was a row of dustbins and a single door, sheet metal with several locks. 'Here we are,' he said.

Harriet got out of the van and as she did so the door opened and a short, fat man came out, dressed entirely in white. The man seemed to be Japanese. He had pale orange skin and slanting eyes. There was a chef's hat balanced on his head. When he smiled, three gold teeth glinted in the afternoon light.

'You got her!' he exclaimed. He had a strong oriental accent.

'Yes. This is Harriet.' Algernon had once again unfolded himself from the van.

'Do you know how much she weigh?' the chef asked.

'I haven't weighed her yet.'

The chef ran his eyes over her. Harriet was beginning to feel more and more uneasy. The way the man was examining her...well, she could almost have been a piece of meat. 'She very good,' he murmured.

'Young and spoilt,' Algernon replied. He gestured at the door. 'This way, my dear.'

'What about my cases?'

'You won't need those.'

Harriet was nervous now. She wasn't sure why but it was not knowing that made her feel all the worse. Perhaps it was the name. Sawney Bean. Now that she thought about it, she *did* know it. She'd heard that name on a television programme or perhaps she'd read it in a book. Certainly she knew it. But how...?

She allowed the two men to lead her into the restaurant and flinched as the solid metal door swung shut behind her. She found herself in a gleaming kitchen, all white-tiled surfaces, industrial-sized cookers and gleaming pots and pans. The restaurant was closed. It was about three o'clock in the afternoon. Lunch was over. It was still some time until dinner.

She became aware that Algernon and the chef were staring at her silently, both with the same excited, hungry eyes. Sawney Bean! *Where* had she heard the name?

'She perfect,' the chef said.

'That's what I thought,' Algernon agreed.

'A bit fatty perhaps...'

'I'm not fat!' Harriet exclaimed. 'Anyway, I've decided I don't like it here. I want to go home. You can take me straight back.'

Algernon laughed softly. 'It's too late for that,' he said. 'Much too late. I've paid a great deal of money for you, my dear. And I told you, we want you here for dinner tonight.'

'Maybe we start by poaching her in white wine,' the chef said. 'Then later tonight with a Béarnaise sauce...'

And that was when Harriet remembered. Sawney Bean. She had read about him in a book of horror stories.

Sawney Bean.

The cannibal.

She opened her mouth to scream but no sound came out. Of course, it's impossible to scream when you're having a bad dream. You try to scream but your mouth won't obey you. Nothing will come out. That was what was happening to Harriet. She could feel the scream welling up inside her. She could see Algernon and the chef closing in on her. The room was spinning, the pots and pans dancing around her head, and still the scream wouldn't come. And then she was sucked into a vortex and the last thing she remembered was a hand reaching out to support her so she wouldn't bruise herself, wouldn't damage her flesh when she fell.

Mercifully, that was when she woke up.

It had all been a horrible dream.

Harriet opened her eyes slowly. It was the most delicious moment of her life, to know that everything that had happened *hadn't* happened. Her father hadn't gone bankrupt. Her parents hadn't sold her to some creep in a white van. Fifi would still be there to help her get dressed and serve up the breakfast. She would get up and go to school and in a few weeks' time she and her mother would leave on their Caribbean cruise. She was annoyed that such a ridiculous dream should have frightened her so much. On the other hand, it had seemed so realistic.

She lifted a hand to rub her forehead.

Or tried to.

Her hands were tied behind her. Harriet opened her eyes wide. She was lying on a marble slab in a kitchen. A huge pot of water was boiling on a stove. A Japanese chef was chopping onions with a glinting stainless steel knife.

Harriet opened her mouth.

This time she was able to scream.

# SCARED

Gary Wilson was lost. He was also hot, tired and angry. As he slogged his way through a field that looked exactly the same as the last field and exactly the same as the one ahead, he cursed the countryside, his grandmother for living in it, and above all his mother for dragging him from their comfortable London house and dumping him in the middle of it. When he got home he would make her suffer, that was for sure. But where exactly was home? How had he managed to get so lost?

He stopped for the tenth time and tried to get his bearings. If there had been a hill he would have climbed it, trying to catch sight of the pink cottage where his grandmother lived. But this was Suffolk, the flattest county in England, where country lanes could lie perfectly concealed behind even the shortest length of grass and where the horizon was always much further away than it had any right to be.

Gary was fifteen years old, tall for his age, with the permanent scowl and narrow eyes of the fully qualified school bully. He wasn't heavily built - if anything he was on the thin side - but he had long arms, hard fists, and he knew how to use them. Maybe that was what made him so angry now. Gary liked to be in control. He knew how to look after himself. If anyone had seen him, stumbling around an empty field in the middle of nowhere, they'd have laughed at him. And of course he'd have had to pay them back.

Nobody laughed at Gary Wilson. Not at his name, not at his place in class (always last), not at the acne which had recently exploded across his face. Generally people avoided him, which suited Gary fine. He actually enjoyed hurting other kids, taking their lunch-money or ripping pages out of their books. But scaring them was just as much fun. He liked what he saw in their eyes. They were scared. And Gary liked that best of all.

About a quarter of the way across the field, Gary's foot found a pot-hole in the ground and he was sent sprawling with his hands outstretched. He managed to save himself from falling but a bolt of pain shot up his leg as his ankle twisted. He swore silently, the four-letter word that always made his mother twitch nervously in her chair. She had long since stopped trying to talk him out of using bad language. He was as tall as her now and he knew that in her own, quiet way, she was scared of him too. Sometimes she would try to reason with him, but for her the time of telling had long since passed.

He was her only child. Her husband – Edward Wilson – had been a clerk at the local bank until one day, quite suddenly, he had fallen over dead. It was a massive heart attack, they said. He was still holding his date-stamp in one hand when they found him. Gary had never got on with his father and hadn't really missed him – particularly when he realised that he was now the man of the house.

The house in question was a two-up, two-down, part of a terrace in Notting Hill Gate. There were insurance policies and the bank provided a small pension so Jane Wilson was able to keep it. Even so, she'd had to go back to work to support Gary and herself...no need to ask which of the two was the more expensive.

Holidays abroad were out of the question. As much as Gary whined and complained, Jane Wilson couldn't find the money. But her mother lived on a farm in Suffolk and twice a year, in the summer and at Christmas, the two of them made the two-hour train journey up from London to Pye Hall just outside the little village of Earl Soham.

It was a glorious place. A single track ran up from the road past a line of poplar trees and a Victorian farmhouse and on through a gap in the hedge. The track seemed to come to an end here but in fact it twisted and continued on to a tiny, lopsided cottage painted a soft Suffolk pink in a sea of daisy-strewn grass.

'Isn't it beautiful?' his mother had said as the taxi from the station had rattled up the lane. A couple of black crows swooped overhead and landed in a nearby field.

Gary had sniffed.

'Pye Hall!' His mother had sighed. 'I was so happy here once.'

But where was it?

Where was Pye Hall?

As he crossed what he now realised was a quite enormous field, Gary found himself wincing with every step. He was also beginning to feel the first stirrings of... something. He wasn't actually scared. He was too angry for that. But he was beginning to wonder just how much further he would have to walk before he knew where he was. And how much further *could* he walk? He swatted at a fly that was buzzing him and went on.

Gary had allowed his mother to talk him into coming, knowing that if he complained hard enough she would be forced to bribe him with a handful of CDs – at the very least. Sure enough he had passed the journey from Liverpool Street to Ipswich listening to *Heavy Metal Hits* and had been in a good enough mood to give his grandmother a quick peck on the cheek when they arrived.

'You've grown so much,' the old lady had exclaimed as he slouched into a battered armchair beside the open fireplace in the front room. She always said that. She was so boring.

She glanced at her daughter. 'You're looking thinner, Jane. And you're tired. You've got no colour at all.'

'Mother, I'm fine.'

'No, you're not. You don't look well. But a week in the country will soon sort you out.'

A week in the country! As he limped onward and onward through the field, swatting again at the wretched fly that was still circling his head, Gary thought longingly of concrete roads, bus stops, traffic lights and hamburgers. At last he reached the hedge that divided this field from the next and he grabbed at it, tearing at the leaves with his bare hands. Too late, he saw the nettles behind the leaves. Gary yowled, bringing his clenched hand to his lips. A string of white bumps rose up, scattered across the palm and insides of his fingers.

What was so great about the country?

Oh, his grandmother went on about the peace, the fresh air, all the usual rubbish spouted by people who wouldn't even recognise a zebra crossing if they saw one. People with no life at all. The flowers and the trees and the birds and the bees. Yuck!

'Everything is different in the country,' she would say.

'You float along with time. You don't feel time rushing past you. You can stand out here and imagine how things were before people spoiled everything with their noise and their machines. You can still feel the magic in the countryside. The power of Mother Nature. It's all around you. Alive. Waiting...'

Gary had listened to the old woman and sneered. She was obviously getting senile. There was no magic in the countryside, only days that seemed to drag on for ever and nights with nothing to do. Mother Nature? That was a good one. Even if the old girl *had* existed – which was unlikely – she had long ago been finished off by the cities, buried under miles of concrete motorway. Driving along the M25 at 100 m.p.h. with the roof open and the CD player on full volume...to Gary, *that* would be real magic.

After a few days lazing around the house, Gary had allowed his grandmother to persuade him to go for a walk. The truth was that he was bored by the two women and, anyway, out in the fields he would be able to smoke a couple of the cigarettes he had bought with money stolen from his mother's handbag.

'Make sure you follow the footpaths, Gary,' his mother had said.

'And don't forget the country code,' his grandmother had added.

Gary remembered the country code all right. As he

ambled away from Pye Hall he picked wild flowers and tore them to shreds. When he came to a gate he deliberately left it open, smiling to himself as he thought of the farm animals that might now wander on to the road. He drank a Coke and span the crumpled can into the middle of a meadow full of buttercups. He half snapped the branch off an apple tree and left it dangling there. He smoked a cigarette and threw the butt, still glowing, into the long grass.

And he had strayed off the footpath. Perhaps that hadn't been such a good idea. He was lost before he knew it. He was tramping through a field, crushing the crop underfoot, when he realised that the ground was getting soft and mushy. His foot broke through the corn or whatever it was and water curled over his shoe, soaking into his sock. Gary grimaced, thought for a moment and decided to go back the way he had come...

Only the way he had come was somehow no longer there. It should have been. He had left enough landmarks after all. But suddenly the broken branch, the Coke tin and the torn-up plants had vanished. Nor was there any sign of the footpath. In fact there was nothing at all that Gary recognised. It was very odd.

That had been over two hours ago.

Since then, things had gone from bad to worse. Gary had made his way through a small wood (although he was sure there hadn't been a wood anywhere near Pye Hall) and had managed to scratch his shoulder and gash his leg on a briar. A moment later he had backed into a tree which had torn his favourite jacket, a black and white striped blazer that he had shop-lifted from an Oxfam shop in Notting Hill Gate.

He had managed to get out of the wood - but even that hadn't been easy. Suddenly he had found a stream blocking his path and the only way to cross it had been to balance on a log that was lying in the middle. He had almost done it too but at the last minute the log had rolled under his foot, hurling him backwards into the water. He had stood up spluttering and swearing. Ten minutes later he had stopped to have another cigarette but the whole packet was sodden, useless.

And now...

Now he screamed as the insect, which he had assumed was a fly but which in fact was a wasp, stung him on the side of the neck. He pulled at his damp and dirty Bart Simpson T-shirt, squinting down to see the damage. Out of the corner of his eye he could just make out the edge of a huge, red swelling. He shifted his weight on to his bad foot and groaned as fresh pain shuddered upwards. Where was Pye Hall? This was all his mother's fault. And his grandmother's. They were the ones who'd suggested the walk. Well, they'd pay for it. Perhaps they'd think twice about how lovely the countryside was when they saw their precious cottage go up in smoke.

And then he saw it. The pink walls and slanting chimneys were unmistakable. Somehow he had found his way back. He only had one more field to cross and he'd be there. With a stifled sob, Gary set off. There was a path of sorts going round the side of the field but he wasn't having any of that. He walked straight across the middle. It had only just been sown. Too bad!

This field was even bigger than the one he had just crossed and the sun seemed to be hotter than ever. The soil was soft and his feet sank into it. His ankle was on fire and, every step he took, his legs seemed to get heavier and heavier. The wasp wouldn't leave him alone either. It was buzzing round his head, round and round, the noise drilling into his skull. But Gary was too tired to swat at it again. His arms hung lifelessly in their sockets, his fingertips brushing against the legs of his jeans. The smell of the countryside filled his nostrils, rich and deep, making him feel sick. He had walked now for ten minutes, maybe longer. But Pye Hall was no closer. It was blurred, shimmering on the edge of his vision. He wondered if he was suffering from sunstroke. Surely it hadn't been as hot as this when he set out?

Every step was becoming more difficult. It was as if his feet were trying to root themselves in the ground. He looked back (whimpering as his collar rubbed the wasp sting) and saw with relief that he was exactly halfway across the field. Something ran down his cheek and dripped off his chin – but whether it was sweat or a tear he couldn't say.

He couldn't go any further. There was a pole stuck in the ground ahead of him and Gary seized hold of it gratefully. He would have to rest for a while. The ground was too soft and damp to sit on so he would rest standing up, holding on to the pole. Just a few minutes. Then he would cross the rest of the field.

And then...

And then...


When the sun began to set and there was still no sign of Gary, his grandmother called the police. The officer in charge took a description of the lost boy and that same night they began a cross-country search that would go on for the next five days. But there was no trace of him. The police thought he might have got in to a car with a stranger. He might have been abducted. But nobody had seen anything. It was as if the countryside had taken him and swallowed him up, one policeman said.

Gary watched as the police finally left. He watched as his mother carried her suitcase out of Pye Hall and got into the taxi that would take her back to Ipswich station and her train to London. He was glad to see that she had the decency to cry, mourning her loss. But he couldn't help feeling that she looked rather less tired and rather less ill than she had when she arrived.

Gary's mother did not see him. As she turned round in the taxi to wave goodbye to her mother and Pye Hall, she did notice that this time there were no crows. But then she saw why. They had been scared away by a figure that was standing in the middle of a field, leaning on a stick. For a moment she thought she recognised its torn black and white jacket and the grimy Bart Simpson T-shirt. But she was probably confused. It was best not to say anything.

The taxi accelerated past the new scarecrow and continued down past the poplar trees to the main road.

# A CAREER IN COMPUTER GAMES

It was just a card like all the others, in the window of his local newsagent, but right from the start Kevin knew the job had to be for him. He was sixteen years old and just out of school and there were two things about him that were absolutely true. He had no experience and no qualifications.

Kevin loved games. His pocket computer had gone to school with him every day of the last year, even though it was against school rules, and when it was finally confiscated by a weary teacher in the middle of a geography lesson (just as he'd been about to find the last gold star in

Moon Quest) he'd gone straight out and bought another one – this time with a colour screen and had spent the rest of the term playing with that.

Every day when he got home he threw his bag into the corner, ignoring his homework, and either booted up his dad's lap-top for a game of Brain Dead or Blade of Evil or plugged in his own for a quick session of Road Kill 2. Kevin's bedroom was piled high with computing magazines and posters. It would also be true to say that he had never actually met most of his best friends. He simply exchanged messages with them on the Internet – mainly hints for games, the secret codes and short cuts.

And that wasn't the end of it. On Saturdays, Kevin would take the bus into London and lose himself in the arcades. There was one, right in the heart of Piccadilly, that was three floors high and absolutely crammed with all the latest equipment. Kevin would go up the escalator with his pockets bulging with one-pound coins. To him, there was no sound in the world sweeter than a brand new coin rolling into a slot. By the end of the day, he would stagger home with empty pockets, an empty head and a dazed smile on his face.

The result of all this was that Kevin had finally left school with no knowledge of anything at all. He had failed all his exams – the ones that he'd even bothered to show up for, that is. University was obviously out of the question – he couldn't even have spelled it. And, as he was already discovering, job opportunities for people as ignorant as him were few and far between.

But he wasn't particularly worried. Since the age of thirteen, he'd never been short of money and he saw no reason why this shouldn't continue. Kevin was the youngest of four children living in a large house in Camden Town, north London. His father, a quiet, sad-looking man, did the night shift in a bakery and slept for most of the day so the two of them never met. His mother worked in a shop. He had a brother in the army. A married sister and another brother training to be a taxi-driver. He himself was a thief. And he was good at it.

For that was how he'd got the money to buy himself all the computer equipment and games. That was how he paid for the arcades in town. He'd started with shoplifting – the local supermarket, the corner shops, the book shop and the chemist in the High Street. Then he'd met some other kids who'd taught him the riskier – but more profitable – arts of car theft and burglary. There was a pub he knew in Camden Town where he could get five pounds for a car radio, twenty for a decent stereo or video camera, and no questions asked. Kevin had never been caught. And the way he saw it, provided he was careful, he never would be.

Kevin had been passing the newsagent on his way to the

pub when he saw the notice. Jobs – that is, honest jobs – didn't interest him. But there was something about the advertisement that did. The 'highest salary and bonus' bit for a start. But it wasn't just that. He knew he was fit. He'd sprinted away from enough smashed car windows and broken back doors to know that. He was certainly enthusiastic, at least when it came to computer games. Of course, he might be wasting his time – if they wanted someone to do programming or anything like that. But…

Why not. Why the hell not?

And that was how, three days later, he found himself outside an office in Rupert Street, in the middle of Soho. He had come to meet a Miss Toe. That was what she had called herself. Kevin had called her from a telephone box and he'd been so pleased to get an interview that for once he hadn't vandalised the phone. Now, though, he wasn't so sure. The address that she had given him belonged to a narrow, red-bricked building squeezed in between a cake shop and a tobacconist. It was so narrow, in fact, that he'd walked past it twice before he found where it was. It was also very old, with dusty windows and the sort of front door you'd expect to find on a dungeon. There was a small brass plaque beside this. Kevin had to lean down to read it.

GALACTIC GAMES LTD

It wasn't a good start. In all the magazines he'd read,

Kevin had never heard of anyone called Galactic Games. And now that he thought of it, what sort of computer games company would be advertising in the window of a newsagent in Camden Town? What sort of computer company would have a crummy office like this?

He almost decided to go. He'd actually turned round and walked away before he changed his mind. Now that he was here, he might as well go in. After all, he'd paid for a ticket on the Underground (even if he had cheated and bought a child's fare). He had nothing else to do. It would probably be a laugh and if nobody was looking he might be able to nick an ashtray.

He rang the bell.

'Yes?' The voice at the other end of the intercom was high-pitched, a bit sing-song.

'My name's Kevin Graham,' he said. 'I've come about the job.'

'Oh yes. Please come straight up. The first floor.'

The door buzzed and he pushed it open and went in. A narrow flight of stairs in a dark, empty corridor led up. Kevin was liking this less and less. The stairs were crooked. The whole place felt about a hundred years old. And all sound from the street had disappeared from the moment the heavy door had swung shut behind him. Once again he thought about turning around but it was too late. A door opened at the top of the stairs, spilling a golden light into the gloom. A figure appeared, looking down at him.

'Please. This way...'

Kevin reached the door and saw that it had been opened by a small, Japanese-looking woman wearing a plain black dress with black high-heeled shoes that tilted her forward as if she were about to fall flat on her face. Her face, what he could see of it, was round and pale. Black sunglasses covered her eyes. And she really was small. Her head barely came up to his chin.

'So who are you?' he asked.

'I am Miss Toe,' she said. She had a strange accent. It wasn't Japanese but it certainly wasn't English. And as she spoke she left the tiniest of gaps between each word. 'I – am – Miss – Toe. We – spoke – on – the – telephone.' She closed the door.

Kevin found himself in a small office with a single desk bare but for a single phone and with a single chair behind it. There was nothing else in the room. The walls, recently painted white, didn't have one picture on them, not even a calendar. So much for stealing, he thought to himself. There wasn't anything to take.

'Mr Go will see you now,' she said.

Miss Toe and Mr Go in Soho. Kevin wanted to laugh but for some reason he couldn't. It was too weird.

Mr Go was sitting in an office next to Miss Toe's. It was like walking through a mirror. His room was exactly the same as hers, with bright white walls; one desk, one telephone, but two chairs. Mr Go was the same size as his assistant and also wore dark glasses. He was dressed in a jersey that was slightly too small for him and a pair of cords that was slightly too big. As he stood up, his movements were jerky and he too left gaps between his words.

'Please, come in,' Mr Go said, seeing Kevin at the door. He smiled, revealing a row of teeth with more silver than white. 'Sit down!' He gestured at the chair and Kevin took it, feeling more suspicious by the minute. There was definitely something odd here. Something not quite right. Mr Go reached into his desk and took out a square of paper: some sort of form. Kevin's reading wasn't up to much and anyway the paper was upside down but as far as he could tell the form wasn't written in English. The words were made up of pictures rather than letters and seemed to go down rather than across the page. It had to be Japanese, he supposed.

'What is your name?' Mr Go asked him.

'Kevin Graham.'

'Age?'

'Sixteen.'

'Address?'

Kevin gave it.

'You've left school?'

'Yeah. A couple of months ago.'

'And tell me please. Did you get good GCSEs?'

'No.' Kevin was angry now. 'Your ad said no qualifications needed. That's what it said. So why are you wasting my time asking me?'

Mr Go looked up sharply. It was impossible to tell with the dark glasses covering his eyes, but he seemed to be pleased. 'You're quite right,' he said. 'Quite right. Yes. Qualifications are not required. Not at all. But can you supply references?'

'What do you mean?' Kevin was lounging in his chair. He had decided he didn't care if he got the job or not – and he didn't want this ridiculous Jap to think he did.

'References from your teachers. Or your parents. Or former employers. To tell me what sort of person you are.'

'I've never had an employer,' Kevin said. 'My teachers would just give you a load of rubbish. And my parents can't be bothered. Shove the references! Who needs them anyway?'

Even as he spoke the words, he knew that the interview was probably over. But there was something about the empty room and the small, doll-like man that unnerved him. He wanted to go. To his surprise, Mr Go smiled again and nodded his head vigorously. 'Absolutely!' he agreed. 'The references can indeed be shoved. Although you have only been in my office for a matter of some twenty-nine-and-a-half seconds, I can already see your character for myself. And my dear Kevin – I may call you Kevin? – I can see that it is exactly the sort of character we require. Exactly!'

'What is this place?' Kevin demanded.

'Galactic Games,' Mr Go replied. 'The finest games inventors in the universe. Certainly the most advanced this side of the Milky Way. We've won many, many awards for *Smash Crash Slash 500*. And our new, advanced version (we call it *Smash Crash Slash 500 Plus*) is going to be even better.'

'*Smash Crash Slash*?' Kevin wrinkled his nose. 'I've never heard of it.'

'It hasn't been marketed yet. Not in this…area. But we want you to work on this game. In this game. And if you're game, the job's yours.'

'How much do you pay?' Kevin demanded.

'Two thousand a week plus car plus healthcare plus funeral package.'

'Funeral package?'

'It's just an extra we throw in – not of course that you'll need it.' Mr Go took out a golden pen and scribbled a few notes on the piece of paper, then span it round so that it faced Kevin. 'Sign here,' he said.

Kevin took the pen. It was curiously heavy. But for a moment he hesitated. 'Two thousand a week,' he repeated.

'Yes.'

'What sort of car?'

'Any car you want.'

'But you haven't told me what I have to do. You haven't told me anything about the job…'

Mr Go sighed. 'All right,' he said. 'Right. Right. Right. Never mind. We'll find someone else.'

'Wait a minute…'

'If you're not interested!'

'I am interested.' Kevin had caught the smell of money. Two thousand pounds a week and a car! What did it matter if Mr Go seemed to be completely mad and if he'd never heard of either the company or the game…what was it called? *Bash Smash Dash*. He quickly searched for a clear space on the sheet of paper and scribbled his name.

Kevin Graham…

But the strange thing was that as the pen travelled across the page, it seemed to become red hot in his hand. It only lasted for a second or two, as long as it took him to form his signature, but no sooner was it done than he cried out and dropped the pen, curling his fingers and holding them up as if to find burn marks. But there was nothing. Mr Go picked up the pen. It was quite cool again. He popped it back into his pocket and slid the sheet of paper back to his side of the desk.

145

'Well, that's it,' he said. 'Welcome to *Smash Crash Slash 500 Plus*.'

'When do I start?' Kevin asked.

'You already have.' Mr Go stood up. 'We'll be in touch with you very soon,' he said. He gestured. 'Please. Show yourself out.'

Kevin was going to argue. Part of him even thought of punching the little man on the nose. That would show him! But his hand was still smarting from the pen and he very much wanted to get out, back on to the street. Maybe he'd walk over to the Piccadilly arcade. Or maybe he'd just go home and go to bed. Whatever he did, he didn't want to stay here.

He left the room the way he had come.

Miss Toe was no longer in her office but the door was open on the other side and he walked out. And that was when he noticed something else strange. The door was glowing. It was as if there was a neon strip built into the frame. As he walked through it, the light danced in his eyes, dazzling him.

'What on earth…?' he muttered to himself.

He didn't stop walking until he got home.


There weren't many people around as Kevin turned into the street where he lived. It was half past three and most of the mothers would be fetching their kids from school or in the kitchens preparing tea. The ones who weren't at work themselves, of course. Cranwell Grove was actually a crescent; a long, quiet road with Victorian terraced houses standing side by side all the way round. About half the buildings belonged to a Housing Association and Kevin's father had been lucky enough to get the one at the very end of the row, three floors high, stained glass in the front door and ivy growing up the side. Kevin didn't like it there, of course. He argued with the neighbours. (Why did they have to get so uptight about their cat? He'd only thrown the one brick at it...) And it was *too* quiet for his liking. Too boring and middle class. He'd rather have had his own flat.

He had just reached the front door when he saw the man walking towards him. He wouldn't normally have taken any notice of anyone walking down Cranwell Grove but there were two things about this man that struck him as odd. The first was that he was wearing a suit. The second thing was the speed at which he was walking; a fast, deliberate pace. He was heading for Kevin's house. There could be no doubt of it.

Kevin's first thought was that this was a plain-clothes policeman. With his hand resting on the key which was already in the lock, his mind raced back over the past few weeks. He'd nicked a car stereo from a BMW parked in Camden Road. And then there'd been that bottle of gin that he had slipped out of the off-licence near the station. But neither time had anyone seen him. Could his face have been caught by a video camera? Even if it had been, how had they managed to find him?

The man was closer now, close enough for Kevin to see his face. He shivered. The face was round and expressionless, the mouth a single, horizontal line, the eyes as lifeless as marbles. The man seemed to have had some sort of surgery, plastic surgery that had left him with more plastic than skin. Even his hair could have been painted on.

The man stopped. He was about twenty metres away.

'What do you...?' Kevin began.

The man pulled out a gun.

Kevin stared – more amazed than actually frightened. He had seen guns on television a thousand times. People shot each other all the time in plays and films. But this was different. This man, this total stranger, was just ten paces away. He was standing in Cranwell Grove and he was holding...

The man brought up the weapon and aimed it. Kevin yelled out and ducked. The man fired. The bullet slammed into the door, inches above his head, shattering the wood.

Real bullets!

That was his first, insane thought. This was a real gun with real bullets. His second thought was even more horrible.

The man was aiming again.

Somehow, when Kevin ducked, he'd managed to hold on to the key. It was above his head now, his fingers still clinging around it. Hardly knowing what he was doing, he turned the key in the lock and almost cried with relief as he felt the door open behind him. He leant back and virtually tumbled in as the man fired a second shot, this one snapping into the wall and spitting fragments of sand and brickwork into his face.

He landed with a thud on the hall carpet, twisted round, jerked the key out and slammed the door. For a moment he lay there, panting, his heart beating so hard that he could feel it pushing against his chest. This wasn't happening to him. *What* wasn't happening to him? He tried to collect his thoughts. Some lunatic had escaped from an asylum and had wandered into Cranwell Grove, shooting anything that moved. No. That wasn't right. Kevin remembered how the man had walked towards him. He had been heading straight for Kevin. There was no question about it. It was him the man wanted to kill.

But why? Who was he? Why him?

He heard the sound of feet moving outside. The man hadn't given up! He was getting closer. Desperately, Kevin looked around him. Was he alone in the house?

'Mum!' he called. 'Dad!'

No answer.

He saw the telephone. Of course, he should have thought of it at once. There was a dangerous lunatic outside and he'd wasted precious seconds when he should have been calling the police. He snatched up the receiver but before he had even dialled the first nine, there was a volley of shots that seemed to explode all around him. He stared in horror. From his side, it looked as if the door was tearing itself apart but he knew it was the man out on the pavement, shooting out the lock. Even as he watched, the door handle and lock shuddered and ricocheted on to the carpet. The door swung open.

Kevin did the only thing he could think of. With a shout, he snatched up the table on which the telephone had stood and swung it round in a great arc. And he was lucky. Just as the table reached the door, the man appeared, stepping into the hall. The table smashed right into his face and he fell backwards, crumpling in a heap.

Kevin stood where he was, catching his breath. He was stunned, the gunshots still ringing in his ears, his head reeling. What was he going to do? Oh yes. Ring the police. But the telephone had fallen when he had picked up the table and there it was, smashed on the floor. There was a second phone in his parents' bedroom but that was no use. The door would be locked. His mother had locked it ever since she'd found him stealing from her handbag.

But there *was* a telephone. A box at the end of the

street. Better to go there than stay in the house because the man he'd just hit wouldn't stay unconscious for ever. Better not to be around when he woke up. Kevin stepped over the body and went out.

And stopped.

A second man was walking towards him and what was odd, what made it all so nightmarish, was that this man was identical to the first. Not just similar – exactly the same. They could have been two dummies out of the same shop window. Kevin almost giggled at the thought – but it was true. The same dark suit. The same plastic, empty face. The same measured pace. And now the man was reaching into his jacket for…

…the same heavy, silver-plated gun.

'Go away!' Kevin screamed. He lurched backwards into the house just as the man fired off a shot, the bullet drilling through the stained-glass window in the front door and smashing a picture that hung in the hall.

This time Kevin was defenceless. He had already used the telephone table and apart from his mother's umbrella there was nothing else in sight. He had to get away. That was the only thing to do. He was unarmed. Defenceless. He had just been attacked by a lunatic and now it seemed that the lunatic had a twin brother.

Whimpering to himself, Kevin crossed the hall and ran up the stairs, stumbling as he tried to keep his eyes on the front door. He was aware of a sudden shadow and then the man was there, stepping into the opening and firing at the same time. The bullet shot over Kevin's shoulder. Kevin screamed and jumped out of the window.

He hadn't opened it first. Glass and wood exploded all around him, almost blinding him as he fell through the air and landed on all fours on the roof below. There was a lean-to next to the kitchen at the top of the garden and that was where he was now. His wrist was hurting and he saw that he had cut himself. Bright red blood slid over the gap between his thumb and first finger. Grimacing, he pulled a piece of glass out of the side of his arm. He was just glad he hadn't broken an arm or a leg.

Because he was going to need them.

From where Kevin was standing – or crouching, rather – he had a view of all the back gardens, not just of the houses in Cranwell Grove but those of Addison Road which ran parallel to it. Here everything was green, precise rectangles of lawn separated by crumbling walls and fences and punctuated with greenhouses, sheds, garden furniture and barbecues. He had no time to enjoy the view. Even as he straightened up, he saw them: half-a-dozen more men with guns, all of them identical to the two he had already encountered. They were making their way through the gardens, hoisting themselves over the fences, marching across the lawns.

'Oh no...' he began.

Behind him, the man who had broken through his front door appeared at the shattered window and took aim. Kevin somersaulted forward and landed on his own back lawn, a fall that knocked his breath away and left him dizzy and confused. The man at the window fired. The bullet whacked into a sunflower, chopping it in half. Kevin got to his feet and ran to the far end of the garden, hurled himself over the fence and tumbled, with a furious yell, into his neighbour's goldfish pond.

He was soaking wet. His shoulder was bruised, his wrist stung from the broken glass, and he was feeling sick and disorientated but sheer terror drove him on. It suddenly occurred to him that from the moment the nightmare had begun, nobody had said a word. There were at least eight men in suits pursuing him but none of them had spoken. And despite the sounds of gunfire on a quiet summer afternoon, none of the residents of Cranwell Grove had come to see what was happening. He had never felt more utterly alone.

Dripping water, Kevin crossed his neighbour's garden and then vaulted over the wall into the next garden along. This one had a gate and he pushed through it, emerging into a narrow alleyway that led back to the road. Limping now – he must have twisted his ankle in the fall from the window – he ran to the end, just in time to hop on to a bus that was pulling out of a stop. Gratefully, he sank into his seat. As the bus picked up speed he looked back out of the window. Four of the men in suits – or maybe it was four new ones – had appeared in Cranwell Grove, and stood in a crowd in the middle of the road. Four shop dummies from C&A, Kevin thought. Despite everything, he felt a surge of pleasure. Whoever they were, he had beaten them. He had left them behind.

And that was when he heard the motor cycles.

They roared out of nowhere, overtaking the four men in suits and pounding up the road towards the bus. There were about nine of them; huge machines, all glinting metalwork and fat, black tyres. The nine riders were dressed in uniform mauve leather, covering them from head to toe. Their heads were covered by silver helmets with black glass completely hiding their faces.

'Oh God...' Kevin whispered.

Nobody on the bus seemed to have noticed him. Despite the fact that he was dirty, his clothes soaked, his hair in disarray and his face covered in sweat, the other passengers were completely ignoring him. Even the bus conductor walked straight past him with a vacant smile.

What was happening to him?

What was going on?

The first of the motor bikes drew level with the bus. The rider reached behind him and pulled a weapon out of a huge holster slung across his shoulders. Kevin gazed through the window, his mouth dropping. The rider had produced some sort of bazooka, a weapon at least three metres long and as thick as a tree-trunk. Kevin whimpered. He reached up to pull the 'Stop' cord. The motor cyclist fired.

There was an explosion so loud that several windows shattered. An elderly woman with a newspaper was propelled out of her seat. Kevin saw her hurtle through the air from the very front of the bus to the back where she landed and cheerfully went on reading. The bus careered to the left, mounted the pavement and crashed into the window of a supermarket. Kevin covered his eyes and screamed. He felt the world spinning round him as the wheels of the bus screeched and slid across the supermarket floor. Something soft hit him on the shoulder and he opened one eye to glimpse an avalanche of toilet paper cascading down on him through the hole that the biker had blasted in the bus. The bus was still moving, drilling through the interior of the supermarket. It smashed through breakfast cereals, dairy products and bakery, skidded into soft drinks and frozen vegetables and finally came to a halt in dog food.

Kevin opened his other eye, grateful that it was still there. He was covered in broken glass, fallen plaster, dust and toilet paper. The other passengers were still sitting in their seats, gazing out of the windows and looking only mildly surprised that the driver had decided to take a short cut through a supermarket.

'What's the matter with you?' Kevin screamed. 'Can't you see what's going on?'

Nobody said anything. But the old lady who had been rocketed out of her seat turned a page and smiled at him vaguely.

Outside the supermarket, the motor cycles waited, parked in a perfect semicircle. The drivers dismounted and began to walk towards what was left of the window. Kevin let out a sob and got shakily to his feet. He just had time to throw himself out of the wreckage of the bus before the whole vehicle disappeared in a barrage of explosions, the bazookas ripping it apart as if it were nothing more than a large red paper box.

How he got out of the supermarket he would never know. In all the dust and the confusion he could barely see and the noise of the bazookas had utterly deafened him. All he knew was that somehow he had to survive. He leapt over the cheese counter – but not quite far enough. One foot plopped down in a loose Camembert and he was nearly thrown flat on his back. There was a door on the other side and he reeled through it, dragging a foot which not only hurt but which now smelled of ripe French cheese. There was a storeroom on the other side and a loading bay beyond that. Two men in white coats were unloading a delivery of fresh meat. They ignored him.

Fresh meat. Suddenly Kevin knew how it felt.

Somehow he made it to Camden High Street, dodging up alleyways and crouching behind parked cars, desperately looking out for men in black suits and men on motor bikes. Three yellow helicopters were buzzing overhead now and somehow, just looking at them, he knew they were part of it too. Perhaps it was intuition. Or perhaps it was the fact that they had 'Kill Kevin Graham' written in red letters on their sides. But he knew they were the enemy. They were looking for him.

He had two more narrow escapes.

One of the bikers spotted him outside Waterstone's and fired off a rocket that just missed him, completely destroying the book shop and littering the High Street with a blizzard of burning pages. He was almost killed a few seconds later by one of the helicopters firing an air-to-ground heat-seeking missile. It should have locked on to Kevin's body heat and disintegrated him in a single, vast explosion, but he was lucky. He had been standing next to an electricity showroom and the missile was confused at the last moment by the electric fires on display. It snaked over his shoulder and into the shop, utterly destroying it and three other buildings in the same arcade and although Kevin was blown several metres away by the force of the blast, he wasn't seriously hurt.

By the time the clock struck nine, there was nothing left in the High Street that you could actually call high. Most of the shops had been reduced to piles of rubble. The bus stops and street-lamps had been snapped in half, pillar-boxes uprooted and prefabricated offices de-fabricated and demolished. And when the clock did strike nine it was itself struck by a thermonuclear warhead, fired by one of the helicopters, and blown to smithereens. At least the mauve-suited bikers were nowhere to be seen. It would have been impossible to drive up Camden High Street in anything but a tractor. There wasn't much street left – just a series of huge holes. On the other hand, their place had now been taken by a swarm of green and silver flying dragons with scorpion tails, razor-sharp claws and search-light eyes. The dragons were incinerating anything that moved. But nothing was moving. Night had fallen and Camden Town with it.

Kevin Graham was squatting in one of the bomb craters. His clothes were rags – his jeans missing one entire leg – and his body was streaked with blood, fresh and dry. There was a cut over his eye and a bald patch at the back of his head where a large part of his hair had been burned off. His eyes were red. He had been crying. His tears left dirty tracks down his cheeks. He was lying underneath a mattress that had been blown out of a bed shop. He was grateful for it. It hid him from the helicopters and from the dragons. It was the only soft thing left in his world.

He must have fallen asleep because the next thing he knew, it was light. The morning sun had risen and everything around him was silent. With a shiver, he heaved the mattress off him and stood up. He listened for a moment, then climbed out of the crater.

It was true. The nightmare was over. The armies that had spent the whole day trying to kill him had disappeared. He stretched his legs, feeling the warm sun on his back, and gazed around him at the smouldering mess that had once been a prosperous north London suburb. Well, that didn't matter. To hell with Camden Town. He was alive!

And he had finally worked out what he had to do.

He had to make his way back into town and find the offices of Galactic Games. He had to tell Mr Go that it had all been a mistake, that he didn't want a career in computer games, that he wasn't interested in *Smash Crash Slash 500*, even if it was the most popular game in the universe. And he believed that now. He just wondered from which part of the universe Mr Go had come.

That was what he would do. Mr Go would understand. He'd tear up the contract and it would all be over.

Kevin took a step forward and stopped.

Overhead, he heard a sound like thunder. For a

moment it filled the air – a strange rolling, booming, followed by a pause and then a metallic crash.

A summer storm?

At the far end of the battlefield, a man in a black suit appeared and began to walk towards him.

Kevin felt his legs turn to jelly. His eyes watered and a sob cracked in his throat. He knew that sound all right. He knew it all too well.

The sound of an arcade.

And someone, somewhere, had just put in another coin.

# THE MAN WITH THE YELLOW FACE

I want to tell you how it happened. But it's not easy. It's all a long time ago now and even though I think about it often, there are still things I don't understand. Maybe I never did.

Why did I even go into the machine? What I'm talking about is one of those instant photograph booths. It was on Platform One at York station – four shots for £2.50. It's probably still there now if you want to go and look at it. I've never been back so I can't be sure. Anyway, there I was with my uncle and aunt, waiting for the train to London and we were twenty minutes early and I had about three pounds on me, which was all that was left of my pocket money. I could have gone back to the kiosk and bought a comic, another bar of chocolate, a puzzle book. I could have gone into the café and bought Cokes all round. I could have just hung on to it. But maybe you know the feeling when you've been on holiday and your mum has given you a certain amount to spend. You've just got to spend it. It's almost a challenge. It doesn't matter what you spend it on. You've just got to be sure it's all gone by the time you get home.

Why the photographs? I was thirteen years old then and I suppose I was what you'd call good-looking. Girls said so, anyway. Fair hair, blue eyes, not fat, not thin. It was important to me how I looked – the right jeans, the right trainers, that sort of thing. But it wasn't crucial to me. What I'm trying to say is, I didn't take the photographs to pin on the wall or to prove to anyone what a movie star I was.

I just took them.

I don't know why.

It was the end of a long weekend in York. I was with my uncle and aunt because, back in London, my mum and dad were quietly and efficiently arranging their divorce. It was something that had been coming for a long time and I wasn't bothered by it any more but even so they'd figured it would upset me to see the removal men come in. My father was moving out of the house and into a flat and although my mother was keeping most of the furniture, there was still *his* piano, *his* books and pictures, *his* computer and the old wardrobe that he had inherited from *his* mother. Suddenly everything was his or hers. Before it had simply been ours.

Uncle Peter and Aunt Anne had been drafted in to keep me diverted while it all happened and they'd chosen York, I suppose, because it was far away and I'd never been there before. But if it was a diversion, it didn't really work. Because while I was in York Minster or walking around the walls or being trundled through the darkness in the Viking Museum, all I could think about was my father and how different everything would be without him, without the smell of his cigarettes and the sound of the out-of-tune piano echoing up the stairs.

I was spoiled that weekend. Of course, that's something parents do. The guiltier they feel, the more they'll spend and a divorce, the complete upheaval of my life and theirs, was worth plenty. I had twenty pounds to spend. We stayed in a hotel, not a bed and breakfast. Whatever I wanted, I got.

Even four useless photographs of myself from the photo booth on Platform One.

Was there something strange about that photo booth? It's easy enough to think that now but maybe even then I was a little…scared. If you've been to York you'll know that it's got a proper, old station with a soaring roof, steel girders and solid red brickwork. The platforms are long and curve round, following the rails. When you stand there you almost imagine that a steam train will pull in. A ghost train, perhaps. York is both a medieval and a

Victorian city; enough ghosts for everyone.

But the photo booth was modern. It was an ugly metal box with its bright light glowing behind the plastic facings. It looked out-of-place on the platform – almost as if it had landed there from outer space. It was in a strange position too, quite a long way from the entrance and the benches where my uncle and aunt were sitting. You wouldn't have thought that many people would have come to this part of the platform. As I approached it, I was suddenly alone. And maybe I imagined it but it seemed that a sudden wind had sprung up, as if blown my way by an approaching train. I felt the wind, cold against my face. But there was no train.

For a moment I stood outside the photo booth, wondering what I was going to do. One shot for the front of my exercise book. A shot for my father – he'd be seeing more of it now than he would of me. A silly, cross-eyed shot for the fridge… Somewhere behind me, the tannoy system sprang to life.

'The train now approaching Platform Two is the ten forty-five to Glasgow calling at Darlington, Durham, Newcastle…'

The voice sounded far away. Not even in the station. It was like a rumble coming out of the sky.

I pulled back the curtain and went into the photo booth.

There was a circular stool which you could adjust for

height and a choice of backgrounds – a white curtain, a black curtain, or a blue wall. The people who designed these things were certainly imaginative. I sat down and looked at myself in the square of black glass in front of me. This was where the camera was, but looking in the glass I could only vaguely see my face. I could make out an outline; my hair falling down over one eye, my shoulders, the open neck of my shirt. But my reflection was shadowy and, like the voice on the tannoy, distant. It didn't look like me.

It looked more like my ghost.

Did I hesitate then, before I put the money in? I think I did. I didn't want these photographs. I was wasting my money. But at the same time I was here now and I might as well do it. I felt hemmed in, inside the photo booth, even though there was only one flimsy curtain separating me from the platform. Also, I was nervous that I was going to miss the train even though there were still fifteen minutes until it arrived. Suddenly I wanted to get it over with.

I put in the coins.

For a moment nothing happened and I thought the photo booth might be broken. But then a red light glowed somewhere behind the glass, deep inside the machine. A devil eye, winking at me. The light went out and there was a flash accompanied by a soft, popping sound that went right through my head.

The first picture had caught me unawares. I was just sitting there with my mouth half-open. Before the machine flashed again I quickly adjusted the stool and twisted my features into the most stupid face I could make. The red eye blinked, followed by the flash. That one would be for the fridge. For the third picture, I whipped the black curtain across, leant back and smiled. The picture was for my father and I wanted it to be good. The fourth picture was a complete disaster. I was pulling back the curtain, adjusting the stool and trying to think of something to do when the flash went off and I realised I'd taken a picture of my left shoulder with my face – annoyed and surprised – peering over the top.

That was it. Those were the four pictures I took.

I went outside the photo booth and stood there on my own, waiting for the pictures to develop. Three minutes according to the advert on the side. Nobody came anywhere near and once again I wondered why they had put the machine so far from the station entrance. Further up the platform, the station clock ticked to 10.47. The minute hand was so big that I could actually see it moving, sliding over the Roman numerals. Doors slammed on the other side of a train. There was the blast of a whistle. The 10.45 to Glasgow shuddered out of the station, a couple of minutes late.

The three minutes took an age to pass. Time always slows down when you're waiting for something. I watched the minute hand of the clock make two more complete circles. Another train, without any carriages, chugged backwards along a line on the far side of the station. And meanwhile the photo booth did...nothing. Maybe there were wheels turning inside, chemicals splashing, spools of paper unfolding. But from where I was standing it just looked dead.

Then, with no warning at all, there was a whirr and a strip of white paper was spat out of a slot in the side. My photographs. I waited until a fan had blown the paper dry, then prised it out of its metal cage. Being careful not to get my fingers on the pictures themselves, I turned them over in my hand.

Four pictures.

The first. Me looking stupid.

The second. Me out of focus.

The fourth. Me from behind.

But the third picture, in the middle of the strip, wasn't a picture of me at all.

It was a picture of a man, and one of the ugliest men I had ever seen. Just looking at him, holding him in my hand, sent a shiver all the way up my arm and round the back of my neck. The man had a yellow face. There was something terribly wrong with his skin which seemed to be crumpled up around his neck and chin, like an old paper bag. He had blue eyes but they had sunk back, hiding in the dark shadows of his eye sockets. His hair was grey and string-like, hanging lifelessly over his forehead. The skin here was damaged too, as if someone had drawn a map on it and then rubbed it out, leaving just faint traces. The man was leaning back against the black curtain and maybe he was smiling. His lips were certainly stretched in something like a smile but there was no humour there at all. He was staring at me, staring up from the palm of my hand. And I would have said his face was filled with raw horror.

I almost crumpled up the photographs then and there. There was something so shocking about the man that I couldn't bear to look at him. I tried to look at the three images of myself but each time my eyes were drawn down or up so that they settled only on him. I closed my fingers, bending them over his face, trying to blot him out. But it was too late. Even when I wasn't looking at him I could still see him. I could still feel him looking at me.

But who was he and how had he got there? I walked away from the machine, glad to be going back to where there were people, away from that deserted end of the platform. Obviously the photo booth *had* been broken. It must have muddled up my photographs with those of whoever had visited it just before me. At least, that's what I tried to tell myself.

My Uncle Peter was waiting for me at the bench. He seemed relieved to see me.

'I thought we were going to miss the train,' he said. He ground out the Gauloise he'd been smoking. He was as bad as my father when it came to cigarettes. High-tar French. Not just damaging your health. Destroying it.

'So let's see them,' Aunt Anne said. She was a pretty, rather nervous woman who always managed to sound enthusiastic about everything. 'How did they come out?'

'The machine was broken,' I said.

'The camera probably cracked when it saw your face.' Peter gave one of his throaty laughs. 'Let's see...'

I held out the strip of film. They took it.

'Who's this?' Anne tried to sound cheerful but I could see that the man with the yellow face had disturbed her. I wasn't surprised. He'd disturbed me.

'He wasn't there,' I said. 'I mean, I didn't see him. All the photographs were of me – but when they were developed, he was there.'

'It must have been broken,' Peter said. 'This must be the last person who was in there.'

Which was exactly what I had thought. Only now I wasn't so sure. Because it had occurred to me that if there was something wrong with the machine and everyone was getting photographs of someone else, then surely the man with the yellow face would have appeared at the very top of the row: one photograph of him followed by three of me. Then whoever went in next would get one picture of me followed by three of them. And so on.

And there was something else.

Now that I thought about it, the man was sitting in exactly the same position that I'd taken inside the photo booth. I'd pulled the black curtain across for the third photograph and there it was now. I'd been leaning back and so was he. It was almost as if the man had somehow got into the machine and sat in a deliberate parody of me. And maybe there was something in that smile of his that was mocking and ugly. It was as if he were trying to tell me something. But I didn't want to know.

'I think he's a ghost,' I said.

'A ghost?' Peter laughed again. He had an annoying laugh. It was loud and jagged, like machine-gun fire. 'A ghost in a platform photo booth?'

'Peter...!' Anne was disapproving. She was worried about me. She'd been worried about me since the start of the divorce.

'I feel I know him,' I said. 'I can't explain it. But I've seen him somewhere before.'

'Where?' Anne asked.

'I don't know.'

'In a nightmare?' Peter suggested. 'His face does look a bit of a nightmare.'

I looked at the picture again even though I didn't want to. It was true. He did look familiar. But at the same time I knew that despite what I'd just said, it was a face I'd never seen before.

'The train now arriving at Platform One…'

It was the train announcer's voice again and sure enough there was our train, looking huge and somehow menacing as it slid round the curve of the track. And it was at that very moment, as I reached out to take the photographs, that I had the idea that I shouldn't get on the train because the man with the yellow face was going to be on it, that somehow he was dangerous to me and that the machine had sent me his picture to warn me.

My uncle and aunt gathered up our weekend bags.

'Why don't we wait?' I said.

'What?' My uncle was already halfway through the door.

'Can't we stay a little longer? In York? We could take the train this afternoon…'

'We've got to get back,' my aunt said. As always, hers was the voice of reason. 'Your mother's going to be waiting for us at the station and anyway, we've got reserved seats.'

'Come on!' Uncle Peter was caught between the platform and the train and with people milling around us, trying to get in, this obviously wasn't the best time or place for an argument.

Even now I wonder why I allowed myself to be pushed, or persuaded, into the train. I could have turned round and run away. I could have sat on the platform and refused to move. Maybe if it had been my mother and father there, I would have done but then, of course, if my mother and father had only managed to stay together in the first place none of it would have happened. Do I blame them? Yes. Sometimes I do.

I found myself on the train before I knew it. We had seats quite near the front and that also played a part in what happened. While Uncle Peter stowed the cases up on the rack and Aunt Anne fished in her shopping bag for magazines, drinks and sandwiches, I took the seat next to the window, miserable and afraid without knowing why.

The man with the yellow face. Who was he? A psychopath perhaps, released from a mental hospital, travelling to London with a knife in his raincoat pocket. Or a terrorist with a bomb, one of those suicide bombers you read about in the Middle East. Or a child killer. Or some sort of monster...

I was so certain I was going to meet him that I barely even noticed as the train jerked forward and began to move out of the station. The photographs were still clasped in my hand and I kept on looking from the yellow face to the other passengers in the carriage, expecting at any moment to see him coming towards me.

'What's the matter with you?' my uncle asked. 'You look like you've seen a ghost.'

I was expecting to. I said nothing.

'Is it that photograph?' Anne asked. 'Really, Simon, I don't know why it's upset you so much.'

And then the ticket collector came. Not a yellow face at all but a black one, smiling. Everything was normal. We were on a train heading for London and I had allowed myself to get flustered about nothing. I took the strip of photographs and bent it so that the yellow face disappeared behind the folds. When I got back to London, I'd cut it out. When I got back to London.

But I didn't get back to London. Not for a long, long time.

I didn't even know anything was wrong until it had happened. We were travelling fast, whizzing through green fields and clumps of woodland when I felt a slight lurch as if invisible arms had reached down and pulled me out of my seat. That was all there was at first, a sort of mechanical hiccup. But then I had the strange sensation that the train was flying. It was like a plane at the end of the runway, the front of the train separating from the ground. It could only have lasted a couple of seconds but in my memory those seconds seem to stretch out for ever. I remember my uncle's head turning, the question forming itself on his face. And my aunt, perhaps realising what was

173

happening before we did, opening her mouth to scream. I remember the other passengers; I carry snapshots of them in my head. A mother with two small daughters, both with ribbons in their hair. A man with a moustache, his pen hovering over the *Times* crossword. A boy of about my own age, listening to a Walkman. The train was almost full. There was hardly an empty seat in sight.

And then the smash of the impact, the world spinning upside down, windows shattering, coats and suitcases tumbling down, sheets of paper whipping into my face, thousands of tiny fragments of glass swarming into me, the deafening scream of tearing metal, the sparks and the smoke and the flames leaping up, cold air rushing in and then the horrible rolling and shuddering that was like the very worst sort of fairground ride only this time the terror wasn't going to stop, this time it was all for real.

Silence.

They always say there's silence after an accident and they're right. I was on my back with something pressing down on me. I could only see out of one eye. Something dripped on to my face. Blood.

Then the screams began.

It turned out that some kids – maniacs – had dropped a concrete pile off a bridge outside Grantham. The train hit it and derailed. Nine people were killed in the crash and a further twenty-nine were seriously injured. I was one of the worst of them. I don't remember anything more of what happened, which is just as well as my carriage caught fire and I was badly burned before my uncle managed to drag me to safety. He was hardly hurt in the accident, apart from a few cuts and bruises. Aunt Anne broke her arm.

I spent many weeks in hospital and I don't remember much of that either. All in all, it was six months before I was better but 'better' in my case was never what I had been before.

This all happened thirty years ago.

And now?

I suppose I can't complain. After all, I wasn't killed and despite my injuries, I enjoy my life. But the injuries are still there. The plastic surgeons did what they could but I'd suffered third-degree burns over much of my body and there wasn't a whole lot they could do. My hair grew back but it's always been grey and rather lifeless. My eyes are sunken. And then there's my skin.

I sit here looking in the mirror.

And the man with the yellow face looks back.

# THE MONKEY'S EAR

The story began, as so many stories do, in the *souk* – or covered market – of Marrakesh. It has been said that there are as many stories in the *souk* as there are products and if you have ever lost yourself in the dozens of covered walkways jammed on all sides with the hundreds of shops and little stalls groaning under the weight of thousands of objects from trinkets and spice bottles to carpets and coffee beans, you will realise that this must add up to more stories than could be told in a hundred-and-one nights or even a hundred-and-one years.

The Beckers had come to Morocco on holiday and had found themselves in the *souk* of Marrakesh only because they had accepted a free tour to go there. All the hotels offered free tours. The idea, of course, was to get the tourists to spend their money once they get to the market. But it wasn't going to work this time…not with the Beckers.

'It's too hot here,' Brenda Becker was complaining. 'And all these flies! We shouldn't have come! I said I didn't want to come. And anyway it's not as if there's any-thing to buy. All this foreign muck...' She swatted at a fly buzzing around her plump, rather sunburned face. 'Why can't we just find a branch of Marks and Spencer?' she moaned.

Her husband, Brian Becker, gritted his teeth and fol-lowed behind her. It seemed to him that he was always one step behind her, like Prince Philip and the flipping Queen. It was certainly true that she ruled over everything he did. That was why he enjoyed his job so much – he worked as a traffic warden. First of all, it got him away from her. But also it meant that, at least when he was out on the road, he was in charge.

A salesman in torn jeans and a grubby T-shirt came up to him, showing off a string of beads. Brian waved a tired hand. 'Go away!' he shouted. 'Sod off, Sinbad!' He stopped and wiped the sweat off his forehead, where it had dripped through what was left of his hair. Brian Becker was a small, weedy man with a thin face and slightly orange skin. He had lost his hair before he was twenty and even now he was embarrassed by the sight of his head, bald and speckled like an egg. That was another good thing about being a traffic warden. He liked the uniform. It made him feel smart, particularly the cap which disguised his baldness. He often wore the cap at home, in bed and even in the bath. But dressed as he was now, in shorts that were much too wide for his spindly legs and a brilliant shirt festooned with flowers (Brenda had chosen it for him before they left) he looked simply ridiculous.

A twelve-year-old boy, walking just beside Arthur, completed the family. This was Bart Becker, their only child. Bart had been fortunate in that he had inherited neither his father's looks nor his mother's excessive weight. He was slim with a pale face and fair hair that rose over his forehead rather like his favourite comic-book hero, Tintin. He was the only one of the three who was enjoying his time in the *souk*. The jumble of colours, the rich smells and the shouts of the traders woven in with the distant wail of pipes and drums all seemed mysterious and exciting to him. Perhaps the main difference between Bart and his parents was that from a very early age he had enjoyed reading books. He loved stories and to him life was a constant adventure. To his parents it was simply something they had to get through.

'We're lost!' Brenda exclaimed. 'This is all your fault, Brian. I want to go back to the hotel.'

'All right! All right!' Brian licked his lips and looked around him. The trouble was that here, in the middle of the *souk*, every passageway looked much like the next one and he had long ago lost any sense of direction. 'It's that way,' he said, pointing.

'We just came from there!'

'Did we?'

'You're an idiot, Brian. My mother always said it and I should have listened to her. We're lost and we're never going to get out of this wretched place.'

'All right! All right!' Brian was forever repeating the same two words. 'I'll ask someone.'

There was a shop to one side selling antique daggers and pieces of jewellery. As Brenda had already pointed out – several times – everything in the *souk* was probably fake. Most of it was no more antique than her own artificial hip. But this stall was different. The knives looked somehow a little more deadly and the jewels glowed just a little more brightly. And there was something else. The very building itself, dark and crooked, seemed older than the rest of the *souk*, as if it had been there first and the rest of the market had slowly grown around it.

They went in. As they passed through the door all the sounds of the *souk* were abruptly shut off. They found themselves standing on a thick carpet in a cave-like room with the smell of sweet mint tea hanging in the air.

'There's nobody here!' Brenda exclaimed.

'Look at this! This is wicked!' Bart had found a long, curving sword. The hilt was encrusted with dark green stones and the blade was stained with what could have been dried blood.

'Don't touch it, Bart!' Brenda snapped. 'It's dirty.'

'And we'll have to pay for it if you break it,' Brian added.

A curtain hanging over a door rippled and a young boy appeared. He must have been about the same age as Bart but he was shorter with very dark skin, black hair and a round, slightly feminine face. He would have been handsome but for the fact that one of his eyes had a large sty, forcing it into a squint, and this made him look almost sinister.

'Good morning. You want buy?' His English was heavily accented and sing-song. He had probably learnt it parrot-fashion from his parents.

'We're not here to buy, thank you very much,' Brenda said.

'We're looking for the way out. The exit.' Brian jerked his thumb in the direction of the door. 'Go to the hotel. Taxi!'

'We have fine jewellery,' the boy replied. 'Nice necklace for lady. Or maybe you like carpet?'

'We don't want jewellery or carpets,' Brian replied angrily. 'We want to go home!'

'This is useless, Brian!' Brenda muttered.

'I sell you something very special!' The boy looked around him and his eyes settled on a wrinkled object lying on a shelf. It was brown and curved, half wrapped in mouldy tissue paper. 'I sell you this!' He took it and placed it on the counter.

'We don't want it,' Brian said.

'It's revolting,' Brenda agreed.

'What is it?' Bart asked.

The boy leered. 'It is my uncle's,' he said. 'The monkey's ear. It is very old. Very powerful. Very secret.'

'What does it do?' Bart asked.

'Don't encourage him, Bart,' his mother said.

But it was too late. The boy ignored her. 'The monkey's ear gives four wishes,' he said. He counted on his fingers as if checking his English. 'One. Two. Three. Four. You say to the ear what you want and you get. Very rare! But also very cheap! I give you good price…'

'We don't want it,' Brenda insisted.

Bart reached out and took it. The ear nestled in the palm of his hand. It seemed to be made of leather but there were a few hairs on the back. The inside of the ear was black and felt like plastic. He rather hoped it was plastic. He didn't particularly want to imagine that he was holding a real ear, severed from a real monkey.

'Four wishes,' the boy repeated. 'One. Two. Three. Four.'

'Let's get out of here,' Brenda said.

'No. I want it!' Bart looked up at his parents. 'You said

I could have something from the *souk* and I want this!'

'But why?' A trickle of sweat dripped off Brian's chin and he wiped it with the cuff of his shirt. 'What do you want it for?'

'I just want it. I think it's cool...'

'Brian...?' Brenda began, using her special tone of voice. She always used it when she was about to explode.

'How much do you want for it?' Brian asked.

'A thousand dirhem,' the boy replied.

'A thousand dirhem? That's...That's...' Brian tried to work it out.

'It's too much,' Brenda cut in. 'It's more than fifty pounds.'

'Will you take five hundred dirhem?' Bart asked.

'Seven hundred,' the boy replied.

'Come on, Bart.' Brian grabbed hold of his son's arm. 'We didn't come in to buy anything. We just wanted to find the way out!'

'Six hundred!' Bart insisted. He wasn't quite sure why he wanted the monkey's ear but now that he had decided on it he was determined to have his way.

'Yes. Is deal. Six hundred.' The boy rapidly folded the monkey's ear in its dirty wrapping and held it out.

Brian grimaced, then counted out the notes. 'That's still twenty quid,' he complained. 'It seems a lot to pay for a bit of rubbish...'

'You promised,' Bart said. He'd actually worked out that the price was nearer thirty pounds but thought it better not to say.

They left the shop and within minutes they had once again disappeared into the swirl of the *souk*. Back in the shop, the curtain had moved for a second time and an enormously fat man had come in, dressed in traditional white robes that reached down to his sandals. The man had popped out to buy some Turkish Delight and was licking the last traces from his fingers as he sat down behind the counter. He glanced at the boy who was still counting the money. The man frowned and the two of them began to talk in their own language so that even if the Beckers had been there they wouldn't have understood a word that was said.

*'Some tourists came in, Uncle. Stupid English tourists. They gave me six hundred dirhem!'*

*'What did you sell them?'*

*'The monkey's ear.'*

The man's eyes widened. He stood up quickly and went over to the shelf. One look told him all he needed to know. *'You sold them the monkey's ear!'* he exclaimed. *'Where are they? Where did they go?'* He grabbed hold of the boy and drew him closer. *'Tell me!'*

*'They've left! I thought you'd be pleased, Uncle! You told me that the monkey's ear was worthless. You said it was...'*

'I said we couldn't sell it! We mustn't sell it! The monkey that the ear was taken from was sick. You have no idea of the danger! Quickly, you son-of-a-goat! You must find the tourists. You must give them back their money. You must get it back…'

'But you said…!'

'Find them! Go now! In the name of Allah, let's pray it's not too late!' The man pushed the boy out of the shop. 'Search everywhere!'

The boy ran out into the *souk*. The man sank back into his seat, his head buried in his hands.

It was already too late. The Beckers had managed to find their way out and were by now in a taxi on the way back to their hotel. And two days later they left Marrakesh. The monkey's ear went with them.


The Beckers lived in a modern bungalow in Stanmore, a sprawling suburb to the north of London. They had been home for a week when Brenda stumbled on the monkey's ear. She was cleaning Bart's bedroom. Brenda had a strange way of cleaning. Somehow it always involved searching every drawer and cupboard, reading Bart's diary and letters and generally poking around wherever she could. She was the sort of mother who always believed the worst of her child. She was sure he kept secrets from her. Perhaps he had started smoking. Or perhaps he was gay. Whatever he was hiding, she was determined to be the first to find out.

As usual though, she had found nothing. She had come upon the monkey's ear underneath a pile of Tintin comics and she carried it downstairs in order to prove a point.

Bart had just got home from school. Brian had also got back from work. He'd had a disappointing day. Although he'd been out in the street for nine hours, he'd only issued three hundred and seven parking tickets, far short of his record. He was sitting in the kitchen, still wearing his uniform and precious cap, eating a fish-finger sandwich. Bart was also at the table, doing his homework.

'I see you've still got this filthy thing,' Brenda exclaimed.

'Mum...' Bart began. He knew his mother must have been looking through his room.

'We paid all that money for it and you've just shoved it in a drawer.' She sniffed indignantly. 'It's a complete waste. We should never have bought it.'

'It's not true,' Bart protested. 'I took it to school and showed everyone. They thought it was creepy.'

'Have you made any wishes?' Brian giggled. 'You could wish yourself top of the class. It would make a pleasant change.'

'No.' Bart had almost forgotten what the boy with the sty had said but the truth was that he would have been too embarrassed to make a wish using the monkey's ear. It would be like saying he believed in fairies or Santa Claus. He had wanted the ear because it was strange and ugly. Not because he thought it could make him rich.

His father must have been reading his mind. 'It's all just rubbish,' he said. 'A monkey's ear that gives you wishes! That's just a load of cobblers!'

'That's not true!' Bart couldn't stop himself arguing with his father. He did it all the time. 'We had a story in school this week. It was exactly the same…except it wasn't a monkey's ear. It was a monkey's paw. And it wasn't as good as an ear because it only gave you three wishes, not four.'

'So what happened in the story?' Brian asked.

'We haven't finished it yet.' This wasn't actually true. Their English teacher had finished the story – which had been written by someone called Edgar Allan Poe – but it had been a hot day and Bart had been day-dreaming so he hadn't heard the end.

Brian took the ear from his wife and turned it over in his hand. He wrinkled his nose. The ear was soft and hairy and felt warm to the touch. 'It would be bloody marvellous if it worked,' he said.

'What would you wish for, Dad?' Bart asked.

Brian held the ear up between his finger and thumb. He raised his other hand for silence. 'I wish for a Rolls-Royce!' he exclaimed.

'What a lot of nonsense!' his wife muttered.

The doorbell rang.

Brian stared at Brenda. Brenda sniffed. 'I'll get it,' Bart said.

He went to the door and opened it. Of course there wasn't going to be a Rolls-Royce there. He didn't expect that for a minute. Even so, he was a little disappointed to discover that he was right, that the street was empty apart from a small, Japanese man holding a brown paper bag.

'Yes?' Bart said.

'This is 15 Green Lane?'

'Yes.' That was their address.

The Japanese man held up the paper bag. 'This is the take-away you ordered.'

'We didn't order any take-away…'

Brenda had come into the hall behind Bart. 'Who is it?' she asked.

'It's someone saying we ordered take-away,' Bart told her.

Brenda glanced at the Japanese man with distaste. She didn't like foreign food and, for that matter, she didn't like foreigners either. 'You've got the wrong house,' she said. 'We don't want any of that here.'

'15 Green Lane,' the Japanese man insisted. 'Sushi for three people.'

'Sushi?'

'It's all paid for.' The man thrust the bag into Bart's hand and before anyone could say anything he had turned and walked away.

Bart carried the bag into the kitchen. 'What is it?' his father asked.

'It's a Japanese take-away,' Bart said. 'He said it was sushi…'

Brian frowned. 'There isn't a Japanese take-away around here.'

'He said it was already paid for,' Brenda said.

'Well, we might as well have it then.'

None of the Beckers had ever eaten sushi before. When they opened the bag they found a plastic box containing three sets of chopsticks and twelve neat rolls of rice stuffed with crab meat and cucumber. Brian picked up one of the pieces with his fingers and ate it. 'Disgusting!' he announced.

'I'll give it to the cat,' Brenda said.

Brian sighed. 'Just for a minute there, I thought that stupid monkey's ear had actually worked,' he said. 'I thought you'd open the door and find I'd won a brand-new Rolls-Royce in a competition or something. Wouldn't that have been great!'

'A Rolls-Royce would be a stupid wish anyway,' Brenda said. 'We could never afford to run it. Just think of the insurance!'

'What would you wish for, Mum?' Bart asked.

'I don't know…' Brenda thought for a minute. 'I'd probably wish for a million pounds. I'd wish I could win the lottery.'

'All right then!' Brian held up the monkey's paw for a second time. 'I wish for a ton of money!'

But nothing happened. The door-bell didn't ring. Nor did the telephone. When the lottery was drawn later that evening (it was a Wednesday) Brian hadn't even got one number right. He went to bed as poor and as frustrated as he had been when he woke up.

There was, however, one strange event the next day. Brian was out on his rounds and had just given a parking ticket to an old-age pensioner and was on his way down to the station where he knew he would find at least a dozen illegally parked cars when he came upon a woman leaning under the bonnet of a small white van. Brian smiled to himself. The van had stopped on a yellow line. He reached for his ticket machine.

'You can't park there!' he exclaimed in his usual way.

The woman straightened up and closed the bonnet. She was young and rather pretty – younger and prettier, certainly, than Brenda. 'I'm very sorry,' she said. 'My van broke down. I'm just on my way to the market. But I've managed to fix it. You're not going to give me a ticket, are you?'

'Well...' Brian pretended to think about it but in fact he had no real reason to ticket her, not if she was about to move. 'All right,' he said. 'I'll let you off this time.'

'You're very kind.' The woman reached into the van and took a small tin off the front seat. The tin had a yellow and black label with the words ELM CROSS FARM printed on the front. 'Let me give you this,' she said. 'To thank you.'

'What is it?' Brian wasn't supposed to accept gifts but he was intrigued.

'It's what I sell at the market,' the woman explained. 'I have a small farm in Hertfordshire. I keep bees. And this is our best honey. It's really delicious. I hope you enjoy it.'

'Well, I don't know...' Brian began. But the woman had already got back into the van and a moment later she drove off.

The honey was delicious. Brian and Bart ate it for tea that evening although Brenda, who was on a diet, refused. She was in a bad mood. The washing machine had broken that afternoon and the repair man had said it would cost ninety pounds to mend. 'I don't know where I'm going to find the cash,' she said. Her eye fell on the monkey's ear that was still lying on the side where they had left it the night before. 'I notice we didn't get a single penny from that stupid thing,' she said. 'If only it did have the power to grant wishes. I'd have a new washing machine for a start. And a new house. And a new husband too, for that matter...'

'What's wrong with me?' Brian complained.

'Well, you haven't got much of a job. You don't earn enough. You pick your nose in bed. And I always think it's a shame you lost your hair. You looked much more handsome when you were younger.'

It was a particularly nasty thing to say. Brenda knew that Brian was sensitive about his appearance but whenever she was in a bad mood she always took it out on him.

Brian scowled. He snatched up the monkey's ear. 'I wish I had my hair again,' he cried.

'You're wasting your time,' Brenda muttered. 'You're bald now and you'll be bald until you die. In fact that ear's got more hair on it than you have!'

That night the weather changed. Although it had been a beautiful day, by the time the Beckers went to bed the clouds had rolled in and the wind had risen and just before midnight there was a sudden, deafening rumble of thunder. Brenda was jerked out of her sleep. 'What was that?' she whimpered.

There was a second boom of thunder. At the same time, the clouds opened and a torrent of rain crashed down, rattling on the roof and driving into the windows with such force that the glass shivered in the frames. The wind became stronger. The trees along Green Lane bent and twisted, then jerked crazily as whole branches were torn off and thrown across the street. Lightning flickered in the air. Somewhere a burglar alarm went off. Dogs howled and barked. The wind screamed and the rain hammered into the house like machine-gun bullets.

'What's going on?' Brenda cried.

Brian went over to the window in his pyjamas but he could hardly see anything. The rain was lashing at the glass, a solid curtain that seemed to enshroud the bungalow. 'It's gone crazy!' he exclaimed.

'But the weather forecast didn't say anything about rain!'

'The weather forecast was wrong!' There was an explosion above Brian's head and something red and solid hurtled past, disintegrating on the front drive.

'What was that?'

'It's the bloody chimney! The whole place is coming down!'

In fact the bungalow stood up to the storm but the following morning at breakfast, the Beckers realised that they were going to have to pay for more than a new washing machine. The storm had torn off the chimney and part of the roof. Brian's car had been blown over on to its side. His rockery was missing. All the fish had been sucked out of his fish-pond and his garden fence was somewhere on the other side of London.

Curiously, theirs was the only house that seemed to have been damaged. It was as if the storm had descended on them and them alone.

'I just don't understand it!' Brenda wailed. 'What's going on? Why us? What have we done to deserve this?'

'It was a blooming hurricane!' Brian said. 'A hurricane! That's what it was!'

Bart had been listening to his parents in silence but Brian's last words somehow reminded him of something. A hurricane? He thought back – to tea the day before, and breakfast before that. He looked at the monkey's ear, lying on the sideboard. His father had made three wishes and nothing had happened.

Or had it?

'It worked!' he muttered. 'The monkey's ear...'

'What are you talking about?' his father demanded.

'It worked, Dad! At least, it worked – sort of. But...' It took Bart a few moments to collect his thoughts. But he knew he was right. He had to be.

'The monkey's ear didn't give us anything,' Brenda said.

'But it did, Mum.' Bart reached out and took it. 'We made three wishes and we got three things – only they weren't the right things. It's as if it didn't hear us properly. Maybe that's why it was so cheap.'

'Twenty quid isn't cheap,' Brian sniffed.

'No, Dad. But if the monkey's ear had been working properly, it would have been a bargain.'

'What are you going on about?'

Bart paused. 'What was your first wish?' he asked.

'I wanted a ton of money.'

'No.' Bart shook his head. 'Your first wish was a Rolls-Royce. And what happened? There was that funny Japanese man at the door and he gave you...'

'He gave us some horrible sushi,' Brenda interrupted.

'Yes. But what are sushi? They're rolls of rice! Don't you see? The ear didn't hear you properly. You asked for a Rolls-Royce and it gave you some rolls of rice!'

'The second wish was a ton of money,' Brenda said.

'That's right. And then you met that woman and she gave you a tin of honey. It was almost the same but it got it wrong a second time. And then, last night...'

'I said I wanted my hair again,' Brian remembered.

'Yes. And what did we get instead?' Brian and Brenda stared at Bart. 'We got a hurricane!'

There was a long silence. All three of them were staring at the ear.

'It's a deaf monkey!' Brian shouted.

'Yes.'

'Blooming heck!' He licked his lips. 'But in that case, if only I'd spoken a little louder...I could have had anything I wanted!'

Brenda's eyes widened. 'You've still got one wish left!' she exclaimed.

Bart snatched the ear. 'But it's my monkey's ear!' he

said. 'You bought it for me and this time I want to make the wish. I can get a new bike. I can never have to go back to school. I can be a millionaire. I want to make the wish!'

'Forget it!' Brian's hand flew out and grabbed hold of the ear. 'We've only got one more chance. I'm head of this family...'

'Dad...!'

'Give it to me!'

'No!'

Father and son were both fighting for the ear while Brenda looked on, still trying to make sense of it all.

'I want it, Dad!' Bart yelled.

'I wish you'd go to hell!'

The words were no sooner out of Brian's mouth than there was a flash and an explosion accompanied by a cloud of green smoke. When Brian and Brenda next opened their eyes, the monkey's ear was lying on the kitchen table. There was no sign of Bart.

Brenda was the first to recover. 'You idiot!' she screeched. 'You nincompoop! What did you say?'

'What did I say...?' Brian remembered his words and his face went pale.

'You told him to go to hell!' She sat down, her mouth dropping open. 'Our son! Our only boy! That was what you wished!'

'Wait a minute! Wait a minute!' Brian thought feverishly. 'You heard what he said! The monkey's ear is broken. It doesn't hear properly.'

'You told him to go to hell!'

Since then, Brian and Brenda Becker have looked for Bart on a hill and in a well. Recently, they moved to the city of Hull and they're almost certain that one day he'll turn up there.

But they haven't found him yet.

# OTHER BLACK APPLES TO GET YOUR TEETH INTO...

WARNING: NOT FOR THE NERVOUS OR FRAIL

*MORE*
# HOROWITZ
## H O R R O R

ANTHONY
HOROWITZ

£5.99

1 84362 789 2

Enter the dark and scary world of

# HOROWITZ  HORROR

and expect the unexpected!

It's a world where everything might *seem* pretty normal. But the weird, the surprising and the truly terrifying are only lurking just out of sight. Like a hitchhiker who isn't quite all he seems, a spooky cottage with a grisly secret and a mobile phone that lets you contact the dead! Each story has a shocking sting in the tale...

*More Horowitz Horror* is a wicked collection of tales of the macabre from acclaimed author and television screen writer, Anthony Horowitz.

Whatever you do, don't take this book
to bed with you...

£4.99

1 84362 204 1

Hard Stew always gets what he wants,
and he wants Davey's new bike.
But Hard Stew's not the only thing bothering Davey,
there's also the big family secret, the one that everyone
wants to keep from him. A secret more frightening
than a hundred Hard Stews.

The sort you've got to stare in the face.
If you've got the guts...

Shortlisted for the Sheffield Children's Book Award.

£4.99

1 84121 306 3

Little Soldier

BERNARD ASHLEY

When Kaninda survives a brutal attack on his village in
East Africa he joins the rebel army, where he's trained
to carry weapons, and use them.
But aid workers take him to London where he fetches up
in a comprehensive school. Clan and tribal conflicts are
everywhere, and on the streets it's estate versus estate,
urban tribe against urban tribe.
All Kaninda wants is to get back to his own war and take
revenge on his enemies. But together with Laura Rose, the
daughter of his new family, he is drawn into a dangerous
local conflit that is spiralling out of control.

Shortlisted for the *Guardian* Children's Book
Award and the Carnegie Medal.

'compelling and unforgettable' – Time Out

£4.99

1 84121 306 3

'Hold on tight!' Tom shouted at the girl. 'Grab hold of the side!'

Tom Welton's never done anything in his life that he's been
proud of...really proud of. But a chance rescue of a girl off
the Suffolk coast seems to offer him the opportunity to
change all that, and soon Tom finds himself risking
everything to save her.

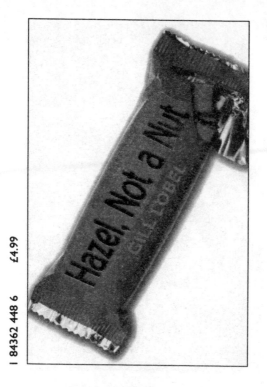

1 84362 448 6  £4.99

Hazel Anne Mooney: Smart. Funny. Fed up. She's unhappy at school, she's far from model-girl slim, and she's being bullied. Lauren Stevenson: Gorgeous. Glamorous. Texting queen. She's pencil-thin, she's perfect. And she's a bully.

A funny and touching story about teenage girls. Perfect to get your teeth into.

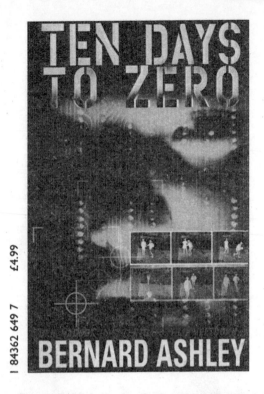

£4.99

1 84362 649 7

When journalist Ben Maddox is thrust full-throttle into an investigation for Zephon TV, he worries that he's in over his head. But as he digs deeper into events, he realises that what's really important is being prepared to fight for what you believe in... and if that means risking his neck, then that's exactly what he'll have to do...

A gripping thriller by the author of *Little Soldier*, short-listed for the CARNEGIE MEDAL and the *GUARDIAN* CHILDREN'S BOOK AWARD.

Nathan's Switch

Pat Moon

£4.99

1 84362 203 3

Nathan is sick of being passed back and forth between his
divorced parents. Then he finds McKay's automatic time dial.
It can switch Nathan back into the past — and the body of
anyone who lived then. It's great for his history homework.
But can it help Nathan bring his parents together again, by
switching him back to when they first fell in love? Can it make
things like they used to be, before his mum walked out?

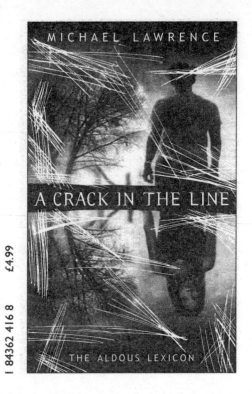

MICHAEL LAWRENCE

A CRACK IN THE LINE

THE ALDOUS LEXICON

I 84362 416 8          £4.99

When Alaric's mother dies in a train accident his world
falls apart. Then one winter's day, Alaric is accidentally
thrown into an alternative reality, a world in which
his mother didn't die and where another girl Naia,
is living his life...

The first book in the acclaimed trilogy
THE ALDOUS LEXICON.

"...a spine tingling thriller about parallel worlds" - The Times

"The complexity of the story-line is not something that
many authors could successfully handle: however
Lawrence has written with a truly cunning hand"
- The Independent on Sunday

1 84362 492 3    £4.99

Thirteen original short stories that get to the very heart
of being thirteen! These award-winning and innovative
authors each write their own unique and compelling
slant on being thirteen. Every story was written
especially for this collection.

# MORE ORCHARD BLACK APPLES

Orchard Black Apples are available from all good bookshops, or can be ordered
direct from the publisher: Orchard Books, PO BOX 29, Douglas IM99 1BQ
Credit card orders please telephone 01624 836000
or fax 01624 837033 or visit our Internet site: www.wattspub.co.uk
or e-mail: bookshop@enterprise.net for details.

To order please quote title, author and ISBN
and your full name and address.
Cheques and postal orders should be made payable to 'Bookpost plc.'
Postage and packing is FREE within the UK
(overseas customers should add £1.00 per book).

Prices and availability are subject to change.